Margaret T Downing

Pencilings and Sketches of the Poets

A Record of Memory and Love

Margaret T Downing

Pencilings and Sketches of the Poets
A Record of Memory and Love

ISBN/EAN: 9783337009885

Printed in Europe, USA, Canada, Australia, Japan

Cover: Foto ©Andreas Hilbeck / pixelio.de

More available books at **www.hansebooks.com**

PENCILINGS

AND

SKETCHES OF THE POETS.

BY

M. T. DOWNING.

———

A RECORD OF MEMORY AND LOVE.

RYE HOMESTEAD, WESTCHESTER CO., N. Y.

———

1867.

James Dickson, Printer, 1, 2, 3 & 4 Tryon Row, New.York.

CONTENTS.

CONTENTS.

PREFACE.

My dear Children:

At length I yield to your reiterated requests, and present in a compact form the little breathings of affection with which my heart has often beguiled itself in addressing you. Valuable only as a proof of maternal affection, they will remind you of the past, while recalling scenes and circumstances now passed away forever—for to each little poem there is a memory known only to ourselves.

The Biographical Sketches," and "Notes, on the Poets," while they were compiled for your ultimate improvement, were thought at the time too advanced for the capacities of all our household band, as their readings have been given to you at different times. The pleasure of novelty is necessarily precluded by a former acquaintance; but instead of this, you will find the tender interest of association, which to your minds will supersede that of talent and ability.

Accept, my dear ones, in the repugnance which I have conquered to comply with your wishes, another evidence of my devoted love.

YOUR MOTHER.

A beautiful picture of the Crucifixion hangs over the altar of St. Mary's, where from our earliest recollections we were used to assemble for divine worship. So dear had it become to us, that we often felt a longing when absent to gaze upon the sad and beautiful lineaments there represented.

> My Jesus, I am sadly gazing,
>   Upon that still, pale form of Thine;
> The thronged worshippers have left Thee,
>   And I alone bend at Thy shrine.
>
> Nearer, still nearer, I approach Thee,
>   Nor pause, till prostrate at Thy feet;
> Refuse me not, my Lord and Master,
>   This commune short, these moments brief.

Here 'neath the shadow of Thy woes,
　I learn the ransom paid for man;
Thine be the school, my heart to teach—
　Thine be the rule, each act to scan.

And thou, sweet Mary, mother, mine,
　On his cold brow thy lips are pressed;
Thy twining arms are 'round Him flung,
　With more than human tenderness.

Oh! by the love thou did'st receive,
　Oh! by the love thou did'st impart,
Obtain for me, I ask no more,
　A refuge in His bleeding heart.

TWILIGHT MUSINGS.

———

'Tis the hour my spirit loves—
  Twilight, with its robes of gray,
With the deeper shades of even,
  Other thoughts and feelings play.

Now I close my eyes to outward,
  Now my soul is turned within,
Welcome, memory, with my dear ones,
  Lead them, softly, gently in.

Once again, those happy faces,
  Smiles and tender looks of love;
Memory, thou hast holy power,
  Traversing the realms above.

I lend me to the sweet delusion,
  And I listen, mother dear,
For the prayers you taught my childhood
  Seem to float upon my ear.

Sister! with the deep, dark eye,
  Sister! with the poet brow,
Thy soft notes at eventide
  Linger, oh! so fondly now.

Mother, sister, absent brother,
  Parted by the deep, blue main,
Shall we ever clasp each other?
  Shall we ever meet again?

Though my present hath its gladness,
  Though my steps are watched by love,
Still I languish for the hour
  When on memory's wings I rove.

Then I hail the pensive twilight,
  And its mantling robes of gray,
With the deeper shades of even,
  Other thoughts and feelings play.

EVENING PRAYER.

FATHER! in this holy hour,
　As the star of daylight fades,
Listen to my heart's low pleadings,
　Grant me Thy support and aid.
Thou hast borne from earliest reason
　With my weak, imperfect will;
Holy Father! guide, sustain me,
　Be my shield and succor still.
In Thy power no ill can reach me,
　In Thy strength no harm befall;
Send Thy blessing to my pillow,
　As I nightly on Thee call.

MEMORIES.

What have I to do with by-gones,
　In my cheerful home to-night,
With my children's happy faces,
　Gleaming in their rosy light?

Why does memory that has slumbered
　Thro' long years of joy and pain,
Bring a presence long since vanished,
　To my vision back again?

Why, when I would rest me quiet,
　In a home replete with love,
Do those scenes so long forgotten,
　All my saddest feelings move?

Who will tell me why I wander
  In the weird land of the past,
Turning from the joy and sunshine,
  Shadows o'er my way to cast?

I mind me of a noble poet,
  Who hath said a word, a tone,
Will recall through scenes dissonant,
  Thoughts we deemed forever gone.

But, away! I will not cherish
  What I would not now recall;
Numberless the many blessings
  Which are shed around us all.

I at least shall learn to prize them,
  And shall praise my God alway,
For the many prayers unanswered,
  That were breathed in life's young day.

So my dear ones, if I wandered,
  For awhile on memory's sea,
Back my little bark has drifted,
  To the home prepared by thee.

JOHANN CHRISTOPH FRIEDERICH SCHILLER was born November 11th, 1759. Fortune placed him in that condition of life which is generally considered to be most conducive to literary eminence—between wealth and penury, neither enervated by the one, nor depressed by the other,—the representative of a station where genius often finds her most favored sons.

His father, JOHANN CASPAR SCHILLER, was a man of an adventurous character; stern, exacting and fond of military glory. At the time of our hero's birth, he held the situation of ensign and adjutant in the Wurtemburg army; still he was fond of his family,

and remarkable for the scrupulous integrity
of his character; but his mother, according
to biographers, was a woman of mild exterior,
with manners peculiarly sweet and gentle—
somewhat grave and serious, perhaps. Her
favorite occupation was to amuse her children with tales calculated to' instruct the
understanding or arouse the fancy; as they
grew older, she repeated to them verses,
which she herself loved and appreciated. In
this early school of maternal affection, the
imagination was developed, and tastes and
feelings awakened in unison with her own.
Like the mother of Lamartine, she early in-
culcated a deep and fervent sense of religion,
by stories and passages from the life of the
Redeemer; often the tears of her little pupils
attested their sympathy and commisseration
and to this early training may be traced the

religious bias which ever marked the character of Schiller, and which showed itself in a
strong predilection for an ecclesastical profession.   This desire remained with him for
many years, and it was with extreme regret
he was obliged to give up what had been his
darling project.   His father, however, had
made different arrangements for his son, and
by placing him in the millitary seminary of
the Grand Duke of Wurtemburg, he virtu-
ally deprived him of the liberty of choice.
Benefits were showered upon his family; his
father was raised to the rank of major, and
young Schiller was promised an appointment
in the Royal service.

A desire from the Duke was equivalent to
a command, and Friederich complied with
the wishes of his father; already he was
learning to sacrifice his own wishes, but the

obedience and affection of a child, while it softened his disinclination, could not entirely smother the keen resentment which the renunciation of his early hopes produced. Intellectual liberty had been his passion; all books not included in the school routine were denied to the students. This only served to increase the desire, and the moments stolen from his severer studies, to be devoted to his favorite authors, were the happiest of his school life. If he had been charmed with Klopstock, he was inspired with Goethe. The teachings of this great master found an echo in the hitherto slumbering thoughts of Schiller, by maintaining that the classical spirit of every nation must be found in the genius of its own romance. This idea, so in consonance with his own belief, formed for him the determination to thoroughly acquaint himself with German literature before he attempted the study of any other. Still the desire to serve God in a religious profession remained dominant in his heart, and he attempted once more to influence his masters by assuring them he was not calculated for the dry study of jurispudenco he was successful only in obtaining as a compromise.

THE PERMISSION TO EXCHANGE MEDICINE FOR LAW.

After passing through a strict course of German poetry, he commenced a translation of Shakspeare, by Wieland.

Hear what he says of the work:

" When I first grew acquainted with this poet, I was indignant with his coldness—indignant with the insensibility which allowed him to jest and sport amid the highest pathos. Led by my knowledge with more modern poets to seek the poet in his works; to meet and sympathize with his heart; to reflect with him over his subject; it was insufferable to me that this poet gave me nothing of himself. Many years had he my entire reverence—certainly my earnest study—before I could comprehend, as it were, his individuality. I was not yet fit to comprehend nature at first hand." Thus in study and contemplation the man's mind developed; long before the genius of the poet manifested itself. But his mental thraldom irritated him; his proud spirit chafed with indignation at the restraints and conventionalities which surrounded him, and he longed to be free.

The elements by which he was surrounded were favorable to the expansion of such an intellect; the time had come when the multitude, of which he was but one, desired most earnestly a leading mind to take the initiative, and setting aside obsolete codes, address himself to men.

In Friederich Schiller they had found such a one, and can we wonder that when the Robbers appeared, by its wild extravagance, its turbulent and mad upheavings, its intense earnestness, was stirred the depth of the German heart, and spreading through inflammable France, rested not until it reached the passionless shores of cold, immovable England, and roused to thought men who had been considered immobility itself?

They beheld in Karl Moor, (the hero of the play,) one whose excess of virtue or exaggerated nobleness, drives him from the habitation of men. His sympathy with the poor

and the oppressed renders him an outcast to
society; in fine he is the martyr of his own
perfections. While the popularity of this
work was dazzling with the masses, its rever-
sion among another class was intense. The
Grand Duke forbade him to write any more poetry, and attend to medicine, (he had recently
been appointed surgeon to a regiment,) or, if
he must write, submit his productions to the
revision of a critic. Imagine the indignation
of Schiller! He writes to a young friend, Karl
Moser:—"So long as my spirit can raise itself
to be free, it shall bow to no yoke." Accordingly he wrote to Freiherr von Dalberg, a noble
man intrusted with the superintendence of the
theatre at Manheim, and the play was to be re-
modelled for the stage. Some of hisfriends at
the same time assisted him in publishing a
volume of lyrics and minor poems, many of
which had been composed some time since.

The success of the Robbers when it appeared on the stage was immense. The play lasted five hours. His audience was drawn from far. They gathered from distant cities, for the fiery rebellion of thought had woke an echo which could not be suppressed. By stealth, in an obscure corner of the house, he witnessed the living embodiment of his own thoughts and passions, and from that time was confirmed in his determination to adopt the vocation to which his genius and his inclinations pointed. Another severe reprimand from the Duke determined him to leave his home; to fly from Stuttgard and throw himself on the world. He confided to his mother the plans for his escape. Fortified by her blessings and her prayers, accompanied by one faithful friend, at the midnight hour he fled from the Capital of Wurtemberg.

The city was illuminated, it was the eve of a grand fete, and by the brilliancy he could distinctly point out the home of his parents. "*O, meine mutter !*" burst from his lips as they wended their lonely way. From this time forward his fame as a dramatic poet con-tinued to increase; he found many difficulties in the way of his advancement, it is true; for some time the Grand Duke continued a show of hostility that prevented Dalberg from affording him his patronage; but this at length was conquered; his manly but respectful in-dependence, his growing fame, the sobering influences of time secured for him an unmo-lested future.

He added to the Robbers, Fiesco, Cabal and Love, Marie Stuart, Joan of Arc, and other dramas of less thrilling interest. He was received with much distinction at court, and the dignity of councillor was conferred upon him by the Duke. At the early age of twenty-six his name had become a household word in Europe. The very misfortunes of his early life had had an ennobling effect upon his manhood, and had served to aug ment the genius of his soul. In his fortunate marriage with the beautiful Charlotte von Lengefeld, every desire of his heart was satisfied. To borrow her sister's pen, (Madame von Wolzogen), "she was highly prepossessing, both in form and face, an expression of the purest goodness of heart animated her features, and her eye beamed only truth and innocence."

A few months after his marriage, he describes his happiness thus: "Life is quite a different thing by the side of a beloved wife than so forsaken and alone, even in summer

I think my very youth will be renewed; an inward poetic life will give it me again." At this time. when he felt the pressing necessity for renewed exertion, to enhance the comforts of his beloved wife, and when his health seemed unequal to the demands which he made upon it, came a letter from Prince von Augustenburg and Count Schimmelman, from which the following is extracted : " We entreat you to receive for three years an annual gift of a thousand dollars. We hear that your health suffers from too severe an application. Do not grudge us the pleasure of contributing to your relief." The effect of this letter on the high-minded Schiller may be imagined. The title of Hofrath, a distinction much coveted, had been bestowed upon him some time before. He was no longer the friendless stripling — the exiled wanderer.

Present one evening at the representation of the "Maid of Orleans," one of those signal triumphs awaited him, which it is seldom the fate of genius to receive. His biographer describes it: "Scarce had the drop scene fallen on the first act, than the house resounded with the cry, *"Es libe Friederich Schiller!"* The cry was swelled by all the force of the orchestra. After the performance the whole crowd collected in the broad place before the theatre to behold the poet. Every head was bared as he passed along; while men lifted their children in their arms to show the pride of Germany to the new generation, crying out: "That is he! that is he!" The Emperor of Austria acknowledged his claims by conferring on him a title of nobility. He was not elated with the honor, and said to a friend who congratulated him:

"It pleases Lolo and my children." His Wallenstein, one of his later productions, bears the impress of wonderful research and profound beauty. Goethe compares it to a wine which wins the taste in proportion to its age. Schiller had now become the national poet of Germany. "The Lay of the Bell," one of his beautiful descriptive poems, followed soon after Wallenstein; in it he thus describes a mother :

"Within sits another—
  The thrifty housewife,
The mild one, the mother;
  Her home is her life,
In its circle she rules,
And the daughters she schools;
  And she cautions the boys
With a bustling command,
And a diligent hand
  Employ'd she employs;
Gives orders to store,
And the much makes the more;"

Locks the chest, and the wardrobe with lavender smell
    ing,

And the hum of the spindle goes quick through the
    dwelling; .

And the hoards in the presses well polished and
    full,

The snow of the linen, the shine of the wool,

Blends the sweet with the good, and from call and en-
    deavor,—rests never!

From this enchanting picture we turn to another. The merry peal that anon ushered in the happy bridal morn, is sadly changed, and—

From the Steeple

Tolls the bell,

Deep and heavy—

The death knell.

Guiding with dirge, note solemn, sad and slow,

To the last home earth's weary wanderers know.

It is that worship'd wife—

It is that faithful mother!

Whom the dark prince of shadows leads benighted,
From that dear arm where oft she hung delighted;
Far from those blithe companions born
Of her and blooming in their morn;
On whom when couched the heart above,
So often looked the mother love!

Ah! rent the sweet home's union band,
And never, never more to come—
She dwells within the shadowy land,
Who was the mother of that home;
How oft they miss that tender guide—
The care, the watch, the face, the mother
And where she sat the babes beside.
Sits with unloving looks—another!

It was said that Schiller's career was one
education, and this is essentially true ; hence
the contrast between his early and his later
works, that wild revolutionary spirit became
moulded and subdued by the sagacious dic-
tates of wisdom and experience.

Friendship, love, assured sympathy—all served to enrich his mind and to mature into perfection his wonderful gifts. As a historian and philosophical writer he ranked high. Hear what Carlyle says : " There never has been in Europe another course of history sketched out on principles so magnificent and philosophical." He says again: "His 'Æsthetic Letters' are the deepest and most compact pieces of reasoning he is anywhere acquainted with." But alas ! when the whole of Europe rung with his fame, the seeds of disease were shortening that precious life; his intellectual activity admitted no repose, while his body was worn to a shadow; his mind grew more and more resolved on action, to thwart him in this was to take away the charm of his existence; as his life neared its close, his meditations on life, nature and eternal providence deepened. " Christianity," he said to his devoted sister-in-law, " has stamped a new impression on humanity, while it revealed a sublime prospect to the soul." Schiller was stricken with his mortal sickness on the 28th of April, 1805; he lingered till the 8th of May, in that state of exhaustion which seemed to preclude all hope. In the decline of that day came on the last struggle. His heart-broken wife knelt by his side, he pressed her hand, when suddenly a nervous tremor came over his frame, the head fell back, a sweet smile lit up his pale face, the world passed away, and in its place was revealed to him the deep unfathomable mysteries of another.

Of the poems of Schiller, those on the elements rank among the first, perhaps equal to them in beauty and perspecuity is Ru-

dolph of Hapsburg. Its design is to depict
the virtue of humility. The story is taken
from an old Swiss chronicle, and Hienrich
says: "The poet has adhered with much
fidelity to the original narrative."

At Aachen in imperial state,
  In that time-hallow'd hall renown'd,
At solemn feast King Rudolph sate,
  , The day that saw the hero crowned;
Bohemia and thy Palgrave Rhine,
  Give this the feast, and that the wine—
    The arch electoral seven!
Like choral stars around the sun,
Gird him whose hand a world has won—
    The anointed choice of heaven!

In galleries raised above the pomp,
  Pressed crowd on crowd their panting way;
And with the joy resounding tromp,
  Rang out the millions', loud huzza;

For closed at last the age of slaughter,
When human blood was pour'd as water,
    Law dawns upon the world!
Sharp force no more shall right the wrong,
And grind the weak to crown the strong
    War's carnage flag is furled.

In Rudolph's hand the goblet shines,
  And gayly round the board looked he,
And proud the feast and bright the wines,
  My kingly heart feels glad to me;
Yet where the gladness-bringer, blessed
In the sweet art which moves the breast,
    With lyre a .d verse divine.
Dear from my youth, the craft of song,
And what as knight I loved so long,
    As Kaisar, still be mine!

Lo! from the circle bending there,
  With sweeping robe the Bard appears,
As silver white his gleaming hair.
    Bleached by the many winds of years;

And music sleeps in golden strings,
Love's rich reward, the minstrel sings,
    Well known to him—the all!
High thoughts and ardent souls desire,
What would the Kaisar from the lyre,
    Amid the banquet-hall?

The great one smiled,—"not mine the sway—
  The minstrel owns a loftier power;
A mightier king inspires the lay—
  Its hest—the impulse of the hour!
As through wide air the tempests sweep,
As gush the springs from mystic deep,
    Or lone, untrodden glen;
So from dark, hidden fount within,
Comes song its own wild world to win—
    Amid the souls of men."

Swift with the fire the minstrel glowed,
  And loud the music swept the ear;
Forth to the chase a hero rode,
    To hunt the chamois deer.

With shaft and horn, the squire behind,
Through greensward meads, the riders wind,
    A small, sweet bell they hear.
Lo! with the host, a holy man,
Before him strides the sacrestan,
    And the bell sounds near and near.

The noble hunter, down inclined
  His reverent head and softened eye,
And honored with a Christian's mind
  The Christ who loves humility.
Loud through the pasture brawls and raves
A brook—the rains had fed the waves,
    And torrents from the hill.
His sandal shoon the priest unbound,
And laid the host upon the ground,
    And neared the swollen rill.

" What wouldst thou, priest?" the count began,
  As marveling much, he halted there;
" Sir count, I seek a dying man,
  Sore—hungering for the heavenly fair.

The bridge that once its safety gave,
Rent by the anger of the wave—
    Drifts down the tide below.
Yet barefoot now, I will not fear
(The soul that seeks its God to cheer)
    Through the wild wave to go."

He gave that priest the knightly steed,
  He reached that priest the lordly reins,
That he might serve the sick man's need.
  Nor slight the task that Heaven ordains,
He took the horse the squire bestrode,
On to the chase the hunter rode,
    On to the sick the priest;
And when the morrow's sun was red,
The servant of the Saviour led
    Back to its lord the beast.

"Now Heaven forefend!" the hero cried,
  "That ere to chase or battle more,
These limbs the sacred beast bestride
  That once my Maker's image bore.

If not a boon allowed to thee,
Thy Lord and mine its master be—
    My tribute to the King!
From whom I hold as fiefs since birth,
Honor, renown, the goods of earth—
    Life and each living thing.

"So may the God who faileth never
  To hear the weak and guide the dim,
To thee give honor, here and ever,
  As thou hast duly honored Him.
Far-famed e'en now through Swisserland,
Thy generous heart and dauntless hand,
    And fair from thine embrace,
Six daughters bloom, six crowns to bring,
Blessed as the daughters of a king—
    The mothers of a race."

The mighty Kaiser heard amazed,
  His heart was in the days of old,
Into the minstrel's heart he gazed,
  That tale the Kaiser's own had told;

Yet in the bard, the priest he knew,
And in the purple veiled from view,
    The gush of holy tears,
A thrill through that vast audience ran,
And every heart the God-like man
    Revering God-reveres.

———

The "Diver," although one of his first ballads, is said to be quite as grand and artistic as those elaborated by his riper genius. A critical writer calls it a lyrical tragedy in two acts, the first act ending with the disappearance of the hero amid the whirlpool; and the conception of the contest of man's will with physical nature, together with the darkly hinted moral not to stretch too far the mercy of Heaven, belong in themselves to the design and ethics of tragedy.

He says, according to the just theory, the main ingredient of terror is the unknown. He here seeks to accomplish as a poet what he before perceived as a critic, and certainly the picture of the lonely diver amid the horrors of the abyss, dwells upon the memory among the sublimest conceptions of modern poetry. The line, "And it bubbles and seethes, and it hisses and roars," struck Goethe in a particular manner, from the power evinced in reflecting truth, though unfamiliar to experience. Schiler had never seen a waterfall.

Bulwer tells us that Schiller modestly owns his obligation to Homer's description of Charybdis.

THE DIVER.

—

"Oh! where is the knight or the squire so bold,
  As to dive to the howling Charybdis below?
I cast in the whirlpool a goblet of gold,
  And o'er it already the dark waters flow;
Whoever to me may the goblet bring,
Shall have for his guerdon that gift of his king."

He spoke, and the cup from the terrible steep,
  That, rugged and hoary, hung over the verge
Of the endless and measureless world of the deep.
  Twirl'd into the maelstrom that maddened the surge.
"And where is the diver so stout to go—
I ask ye again—to the deep below?"

And the knights and the squires that gather'd around,
  Stood silent, and fixed on the ocean their eyes;

They look'd on the dismal and savage profound,
  And the peril chilled back every thought of the prize,
And thrice spoke the monarch, "The cup to win,
Is there never a wight who will venture in?"

And all as before heard in silence the king—
  Till a youth, with an aspect unfearing, but gentle,
M'd the tremulous squires, stepp'd out from the ring.
  Unbuckling his girdle, and doffing his mantle;
And the murmuring crowd, as they parted asunder,
On the stately boy cast their looks of wonder.

As he strode to the marge of the summit, and gave
  One glance on the gulf of that merciless main;
Lo! the wave that forever devours the wave,
  Casts roaringly up the Charybdis again;
And, as with the swell of the far thunder-boom,
Rushes foamingly forth to the heart of the gloom.

And it bubbles and seethes, and it hisses and roars,
  As when fire is with water commix'd and contending;

And the spray of its wrath to the welkin up-soars,
  And flood upon flood hurries on, never ending;
And it never *will* rest, nor from travail be free,
Like a sea that is laboring the birth of a sea.

Yet at length comes a lull o'er the mighty commotion,
  As the whirlpool sucks into black smoothness the swell
Of the white foaming breakers, and cleaves through the
    ocean
  A path that seems winding in darkness to Hell.
Round and round whirl'd the waves, deep and deeper
    still driven,
Like a gorge through the mountainous main thunder-
    riven!

The youth gave his trust to his Maker! before
  That path through the riven abyss closed again—
Hark! a shriek from the crowd rang aloft from the shore,
  And behold! he is whirl'd in the grasp of the main!
And o'er him the breakers mysteriously roll'd,
And the giant-mouth closed on the swimmer so bold.

O'er the surface grim silence lay dark; but the crowd
  Heard the wail from the deep murmer hollow and fell;

They hearken and shudder, lamenting aloud—
  "Gallant youth—noble heart—fare thee well, fare thee
    well!"
More hollow and more wails the deep on the ear—
More dread and more dread grows suspense in its fear.

If thou should'st in those waters thy diadem fling,
  And cry, "Who may find it shall win it and wear,"
God wot, though the prize were the crown of a king—
  A crown at such hazard were valued too dear;
For never shall lips of the living reveal
What the deeps that howl yonder in terror conceal.

Oh! many a bark, to that breast grappled fast,
  Has gone down to the fearful and fathomless grave;
Again, crash'd together the keel and the mast,
  To be seen, toss'd aloft, in the glee of the wave;
Like the growth of a storm ever louder and clearer,
Grows the roar of the gulf rising nearer and nearer.

And it bubbles and seethes, and it hisses and roars,
  As when fire is with water commix'd and contending;

And the spray of its wrath to the welkin up-soars,
  And flood upon flood hurries on, never ending;
And as with the swell of the far thunder-boom,
Rushes roaringly forth from the heart of the gloom.

    *   *   *   *   *   *   *

And lo! from the heart of that far-floating gloom,
  What gleams on the darkness so swan-like and white?
Lo! an arm and a neck, glancing up from the tomb!
  They battle—the man's with the element's might.
It is he! it is he! in his left hand behold,
As a sign, as a joy, shines the goblet of gold!

And he breathed deep, and he breathed long,
  And he greeted the heavenly delight of the day;
They gaze on each other—they shout as they throng,
  "He lives!—lo, the ocean has rendered its prey!
And safe from the whirlpool, and free from the grave,
Comes back to the daylight the soul of the brave!"

And he comes with the crowd in the clamor and glee,
  And the goblet his daring has won from the water,

Ho lifts to the king as he sinks on his knee: ,
  And the king from her maidens has beckon'd his
    daughter;
She pours to the boy the bright wine which they bring,
And thus spake the Diver: "Long life to the king!"

Happy they whom the rose-hues of daylight rejoice,
  The air and the sky that to mortals are given;
May the horror below never more find a voice—
  Nor man stretch too far the wide mercy of Heaven!
Never more—never more may he lift from the sight
The veil which is woven with Terror and Night!

"Quick, brightening like lightening, it tore me along,
  Down, down, till a gush of a torrent, at play
In the rocks of its wilderness, it caught me; and strong
  As the wings of an eagle, it whirl'd me away.
Vain, vain was my struggle—the circle had won me,
Round and round in its dance, the wild elements spun me.

"And I called on my God, and my God heard my prayer,
  In the strength of my need, in the gasp of my breath,

And show'd me a crag that rose up from the lair,
  And I clung to it, nimbly, and baffled the death!
And safe in the perils around me, behold
On the spikes of the coral the goblet of gold.

"Below, at the foot of that precipice drear,
  Spread the gloomy, and purple, and pathless obscure!
A silence of Horror that slept on the ear,
  That the eye more appall'd might the hour endure!
Salamander, snake, dragon, vast reptiles that dwell
  In the deep, coil'd about the grim jaws of their Hell.

"Dark, crawl'd, glided the unspeakable swarms,
  Clamp'd together in masses, misshapen and vast;
Here clung and here bristled the fathomless forms,
  Here the dark, moving bulk of the hammer-fish pass'd;
And with teeth grinning white, and a menacing motion,
Went the terrible shark—the hyena of ocean.

"There I hung, and the awe gather'd icily o'er me,
  So far from the earth, where man's help there was none;
The one human thing, with the goblins before me,
  Alone, in a loneliness so ghastly—*alone!*

Fathom-deep from man's eye in the speechless profound,
With the death of the main and the monsters around.

"Methought, as I gazed through the darkness, that now
   It saw—the dread hundred-limbed creature—its prey!
And darted, O God! from the far-flaming bough
   Of the coral, I swept on the horrible way;
And it seized me, the wave with its wrath and its roar,
It seized me to save—king, the danger is o'er!

On the youth gazed the monarch, and marvell'd; quoth he:
   "Bold Diver, the goblet I promised is thine,
And this ring will I give, a fresh guerdon to thee—
   Never jewels more precious shone up from the mine;
If thou'lt bring me fresh tidings, and venture again,
To say what lies hid in the *innermost* main!"

Then out spake the daughter in tender emotion:
   "Ah! father, my father, what more can there rest?
Enough of this sport with the pitiless ocean—
   He has served thee as none would, thyself hast confess'd;
If nothing can shake thy wild thirst of desire,
Let thy knights put to shame the exploit of the squire!"

The king seized the goblet, he swung it on high,
  And whirling, it fell in the roar of the tide;
"But bring back that goblet again to my eye,
  And I'll hold thee the dearest that rides by my side;
And thine arms shall embrace, as thy bride, I decree,
The maiden whose pity now pleadeth for thee."

In his heart, as he listened, there leap'd the wild joy,
  And the hope and the love through his eyes spoke in fire,
On that bloom, on that blush, gazed delighted the boy;
  The maiden, she faints at the feet of her sire!
Here the guerdon divine, there the danger beneath;
He resolves! to the strife with the life and the death!

They hear the loud surges sweep back in their swell.
  Their coming the thunder-sound heralds along!
Fond eyes yet are tracking the spot where he fell,
  They come, the wild waters, in tumult and throng;
Roaring up to the cliff, roaring back, as before,
But no wave ever brings the lost youth to the shore.

TO M. A. D.

Not wholly dark thy present lot,
　　Though joy her golden wing hath furled,
For where the present cannot reach,
　　Like radiance from another world,
A spirit guides of potent power,
　　That moulds each purpose of the heart—
　　　　The memories of a bygone hour!

Thy bark may float on summer seas,
　　Or lashed by furious waves be driven;
Alike to thee, the whirling storm,
　　Or soft and gentle breeze of even;
Calmly amid the ills of life,
　　Nerved for the strife whate'er it be,
The venture lost, was vantage gained,
　　Though sad the dower it brought to thee.

Not wholly sad, for golden gleams—
  Like those that light the hills at eve,
The reflex of an early dream,
  Which now no longer can deceive,
Illumes the page where time records
  His measured worth of smiles and tears;
For seen thro' his dissolving glass,
  The sadness ever more endears.

Then let us gather up the shreds,
  And garner up the golden sheaves,
For every blossom of the past,
  A soul distilling fragrance leaves;
Not all bereft, for these are thine,
  A measured boon to mortals given—
To temper joy, to chasten woe,
  And fit the wearied soul for Heaven.

SONG.

DEDICATED TO FANNY.

———

Oh! say not that my heart forgets,
   Though silent years have fled,
Since thou, my first and early love,
   Wert numbered with the dead.

My soul has kept its vigils long,
   Through scenes of joy and woe;
One yearning thought of other days,
   Pursues where're I go.

To night the stars are looking down
   Upon the summer sea,
And I am thinking of the time
   I wandered, love, with thee.

4

Oh! sacred past of buried hopes,
  Your mournful memories sweep,
In tender echoes through my soul,
  And lone and sad I weep.

MISS ADELAIDE A. PROCTOR.

———

ADELAIDE A. PROCTOR, the daughter of Barry Cornwall, of whom as yet the world knows so little, sends us a memorial of her life in a volume of poems, so exquisitely tender, so filled with beautiful thoughts, that it is a difficult task to select one having a pre-eminence over another. Like her father, she possessed an easy flow of verse. But under the apparent unconsciousness of critical barriers and rules of diction, there is a flowery grace and a captivating ease that charms and fascinates the reader; her periods are so musical, her imagery so fine. But transcending all this, her sublimity of faith, her dependence on the Great Father is so apparent that we seat ourselves reverently at her young feet, and yield to the inspiration which falls from her lips. A few extracts from "The Parting" tells her story (of a deceived but not broken heart) so truthfully that it seems like a key unlocking the innermost recesses of her soul :

"Without one bitter feeling let us part;
  And for the years in which your love has shed
  A radiance like a glory round my head,
I thank you, yes, I thank you from my heart.

"I thank you, and no grief is in these tears;
  I thank you not in bitterness but truth,
  For the fair vision that adorned my youth
And glorified so many happy years.

"I thank you that your hand dashed down the shrine
   Wherein my idol worship I had paid,
   Else had I never known a soul was made
To serve and worship only the Divine.

"I thank you for a terrible awaking,
   And if reproach seemed hidden in my pain,
   And sorrow seemed to cry on your disdain,
Know that my blessing lay in your forsaking,

" Farewell forever! now in peace we part,
   And should an idle vision of my tears,
   Arise before your soul in after years,
Remember that I thank you from my heart."

As sentiment is the characteristic of
Proctor, so it is remarkably developed in his
daughter, with this great difference : his
portraiture seems almost a deification of a
human passion ; hers are always held in
relationship to the Great Father.   That
which was her greatest joy becomes her

discipline. She bows in meek submission to the chastening rod ; calmly and even hope·fully she takes up the cross, feeling and knowing that "better than the seen lies hid," she is repaid, a light, a new revelation of beauty breaks upon her soul, and she says :

"I thank Thee, Lord, that Thou hast kept
  The best in store,
To have enough, yet not too much
  To long for more;
A yearning for a deeper peace,
  Not known before.

"I thank Thee, Lord, that here our souls,
  Though amply blest,
Can never find, although they seek,
  A perfect rest—
Nor ever shall until they lean
  On Jesus' breast."

Poetry is said to be capricious in its alliances, giving herself alike to the grave and gay, the gentle and the stern. Though this is eminently true, yet she is ever constant to the phases of her possessor. She echoes in her mirth and mourns in her sorrow. She weaves her fragments and conceits for babyhood, and she mourns with us o'er "our dead." Listen to the following:

"How the children leave us, and no traces
    Linger of that smiling angel band;
Gone, forever gone, and in their places
    Weary men and anxious women stand.

"Yet we have some little ones still ours,
    They have kept the baby smile we know,
Which we kissed one day and hid with flowers
    On their dead white faces long ago.

"Only the dead hearts forsake us never;
  Death's last kiss has been the mystic sign,
Consecrating love our own forever,
  Crowning it eternal and divine."

Again she gives us high and holy truth in language of added efficacy and power. The true philosophy of life is couched in the following :

Sow and look onward, upward,
  Where the starry light appears,
Where, in spite of the coward's doubting,
  Or your own heart's trembling fears,
You shall reap in joy the harvest
  . You have sown to day in tears."

And again :

"Pray, though the gift you ask for
  May never comfort your fears,
May never repay your pleadings,
  Yet pray, and with hopeful tears;

And an answer not that you long for,
  But diviner will come one day,
Your eyes are too dim to see it,
  Yet strive to watch and pray."

" Learn that each duty makes its claim
  Upon one soul: not each on all;
How, if God speaks thy brother's name,
  Dare thou make answer to the call?

" The greater peril in the strife,
  The less this evil should be done,
For as in battle so in life,
  Danger and honor still are one."

Who would not learn from such an evan-
gel? It was said of Byron : " that in seeking an ocean for the river of his thoughts,
he bore all hearts along in the rash bewildering emotion." Adelaide Proctor bears
us not along but upward. She nerves us

for the battle of life with lessons wrung from her own heart's experience. She lays bare the secret wounds of her soul, to show us where light entered. If we saunter with her through flowery dells and delicious groves, she allows us not to be captivated by the mere surroundings, beautiful as they may be. Her mind evolves an idea, a comparison or a moral. Showing these are but the faintest corruscations of that light divine, and without which all is nothing. And yet in this relationship there is not sadness, but holy and submissive faith.

'Twas hers

> "To drink the golden spirit of the day
> And triumph in existence."

Truly, did she not collect the shadows of

life into a portentous array? She might have said

> "Fresh hopes are hourly sown
> In furrowed brows."

But kindling aspirations they, that write no wrinkles on the soul.

"The Requital," we call the joy of our household :

> "Loud roared the tempest,
>   Fast fell the sleet;
> A little child angel
>   Passed down the street,
> With trailing pinions
>   And weary feet.

"The moon was hidden,
No stars were bright,
So she could not shelter
In Heaven that night,
For the angel's ladders,
Are rays of light.

"She beat her wings
At each window pane,
And pleaded for shelter,
But all in vain.
Listen, they said,
To the pelting rain.

"She sobbed, as the laughter
And mirth grew higher,
Give me rest and shelter
Beside your fire,
And I will give you
Your heart's desire.

"The Dreamer sat watching
   His embers gleam,
While his heart was floating
   Down hope's bright stream,
So he wove her wailing
   Into his dream.

"But fiercer the tempest
   Rose than before,
When the angel paused
   At an humble door,
And asked for shelter
   And rest once more.

"A weary woman,
   Pale, worn and thin,
With the brand upon her
   Of want and sin,
Heard the child angel
   And took her in.

> "Took her in gently,
>   And did her best
> To dry her pinions,
>   And made her rest
> With tender pity,
>   Upon her breast.

> "When the eastern morning
>   Grew bright and red,
> Up the first sunbeam
>   The angel fled;
> Having kissed the woman
>   And left her—dead."

It might be thought a difficult task for one of high and lofty aspirations to suit herself to the capacity of childhood, but such was the universality of Miss Proctor's genius, that whether we consider her breathing strains for babyhood, or teaching lessons of sublime endurance for poor, suffer ing humanity, we must still accord to her the homage of our heartfelt admiration. What a felicity of expression do we find in the following sweet little fragments:

> "Is my darling tired already,
>   Tired of her day of play!
> Draw your little stool beside me,
>   Smoothe the tangled hair away.
> Can she put the logs together
>   Till they make a cheerful blaze?
> Shall her blind old uncle tell her
>   Something of his youthful days?"

The story is continued with all the winning sweetness which the preface indicates. Another:

> "Will she come to me, little Effie,
>   Will she come, in my arms to rest,
> And nestle her head on my shoulder
>   While the sun goes down in the west?

"I and Effie will sit together,
　All alone in this great arm-chair.
It is silly to mind it, darling,
　When life is so hard to bear.

" While her little soft arms grow tighter
　Round my neck in their clinging hold,
Well—I must not cry on your hair, dear,
　For my tears might tarnish the gold.

"But my Effie won't reason, will she,
　Or endeavor to understand?
Only holds up her mouth to kiss me,
　As she strokes my face with her hand.

*　　*　　*　　*　　*　　*　　*　　*

"But hark!—there is nurse calling Effie;
　It is bed-time, so run away,
And I must go back, or the others
　Will be wondering why I stay.

"So good-night to my darling Effie,
    Be happy, sweetheart, and grow wise;
There's one kiss for her golden ringlets,
    And two for her sleepy eyes."

The style of the above is very much like
Mary Howitt's "My Little Minnie," only
immeasurably superior. That they have
a fascination for children I can answer, for
I have known little ones to perform disagreeable duties with alacrity and pleasure
for the promise that mamma would read
them Miss Proctor, and in a little time, so
much are those poems in consonance with
their tastes and feelings, they could repeat
them readily from memory. I think it was
Beranger who said: "I care not who writes
the sermons of a nation, so I may give
them their songs." But here is one who
combines both. The poem of Fidelis con-

tains such loyalty to friendship and memory
that I cannot forbear inserting some passages:

> "You have taken back the promise
>   That you spoke so long ago—
> Taken back the heart you gave me,
>   I must even let it go.
> Where Love once has breathed Pride dieth,
>   So I struggled but in vain,
> First to keep the links together,
>   Then to piece the broken chain.

> "But it might not be—so freely
>   All your friendship I restore,
> And the heart that I had taken
>   As my own forever more.
> No shade of reproach shall touch you,
>   Dread no more a claim from me—
> But I will not have you fancy
>   That I count myself as free.

"I am bound by the old promise—
  What can break that golden chain?
Not even the words that you have spoken,
  Or the sharpness of my pain.
Do you think, because you fail me,
  And draw back your hand to day,
That from out the heart I gave you,
  My strong love can fade away?

"It will live. No eyes may see it.
  In my soul it will lie deep,
Hidden from all; but I shall feel it
  Often stirring in its sleep.
So, remember, that the friendship
  Which you now think poor and vain,
Will endure, in hope and patience,
  Till you ask for it again."

To those who have compromised their
fidelity, these beautiful lines must be a
stinging remorse. The consciousness of

wasted affection cannot overcome or subdue the true and loyal heart. The line

"Where Love once has breathed Pride dieth,"

reveals the source from whence magnanimity draws its strength.

Theodore Tilton says, in speaking of Mrs. Browning: "Her resemblance to other poets in style and thought are not infrequent." As one evidence he gives us a line from "Lady Geraldine: "

"With a rushing stir uncertain, in the air, the purple curta'n,"

as like a line in "Poe's Raven: "

"And the silken, sad, uncertain rustling of each purple curtain."

These duplicated thoughts we often find among our classic writers. But we are now

going to consider a case where the analogy
is more complete — where plan, incident,
and the expression of sentiment are almost
the same. I allude to the poem of " Enoch
Arden," by Tennyson, and the " Homeward
Bound," by Adelaide Proctor. In both the
story is similar. The hero in each case
leaves wife and children to traverse the
trackless ocean — one is cast away on a
desert island, the other off the "Red Al-
giers," and becomes the slave of the "Black
Moses of Barbary." Enoch Arden, on his
lonely isle, dreams of

> "The babies, their babble, Annie, the small house,
> The climbing street, the mill, the leafy lanes,
> The peacock, yew tree, and the lonely hall,
> The horse he drove, the boat he sold, the chill
> November dawns, and dewy glooming downs,
> The gentle shower, the smell of dying leaves,
> And the low moan of leaden-colored seas."

The hero in "Homeward Bound" sees

> "A fair face, but pale with sorrow,
>   With blue eyes brimful of tears,
> And the little red mouth quivering
>   With a smile to hide its fears.

> "Then I saw, as night grew darker,
>   How she taught my child to pray,
> Holding its small hands together,
>   For its father far away;
> And I felt her sorrow weighing
>   Heavier on me than mine own,
> Pitying her blighted spring-time
>   And her joy so early flown."

After many long and wearisome years both
are freed. They who had been accounted
dead return again to their native land.
One thus describes it:

"It was evening in late autumm,
  And the gusty wind blew chill,
Autumn leaves were falling round me,
  And the red sun lit the hill.

"She was seated by the fire,
  In her arms she held a child,
Whispering baby words caressing,
  And then looking up she smiled—
Smiled on him who stood beside her,
  Oh, the bitter truth was told!
In her look of trusting fondness
  I had seen the look of old.

"But she rose and turned towards me,
  (Cold and dumb I waited there,)
With a shriek of fear and terror,
  And a white face of despair.
He had been an ancient comrade.
  Not a single word we said,
While we gazed upon each other,
  He the living : I the dead.

"Bitter tears that desolate moment,
Bitter tears we wept,
We three broken hearts together,
While the baby smiled and slept.

"Then at last I rose, and turning,
Wrung his hand, but made no sign,
And I stooped and kissed her forehead,
Once more, as if she were mine,
Nothing of farewell I uttered,
Save in broken words to pray
That God would ever guard and bless her—
Then in silence passed away."

Enoch Arden nears his home:

"His eyes upon the stone, he reached the home
Where Annie lived and loved him, and his babes.
In those far seven happy years, were born;
But finding neither light nor murmur there.
A bill of sale gleamed through the drizzle, crept
Still downward, thinking dead or dead to me,
Down to the pool and narrow wharf he went,
Seeking a tavern which of old he knew."

Here Miriam Lane, not knowing him, so brown and bowed, tells him the story of his house:

"How Philip (his old friend) put his little ones to school,
And kept them in it—his long wooing—
Her slow consent, and marriage—the birth
Of Philip's child; and o'er his countenance
No shadow past, nor motion; any one
Regarding well, had deemed he felt the tale
Less than the teller; only when she closed,
Enoch, poor man, was cast away and lost;
He, shaking his grey head pathetically,
Repeated, muttering, cast away and lost;
Again, in deeper inward whispers—lost!"

Here occurs a slight divergence in the comparison. Enoch Arden "does not leave forever," but forms the resolution in his mind to remain near his wife and children yet never let them know of his return,

satisfied that those he loved were happy
in their ignorance of him:

"But Enoch yearned to see her face again.
If I might look on her sweet face again
And know that she is happy!"

The thought drives him forth. And Enoch
saw

"Philip, the slighted suitor of old times,
Stout, rosy, with his babe upon his knees.
And o'er her second father stoopt a girl,
A later but a loftier Annie Lee,
Fair-haired and tall, and from her lifted hand
Dangled a length of ribbon and a ring,
To tempt the babe who reared its creasy arms,
Caught at and ever missed it, and they laughed.
And on the left hand of the hearth he saw
The mother, glancing often toward her babe,
But turning now and then to speak with him,
Her son, who stood beside her tall and strong,
And saying that which pleased him, for he smiled.

"Then he, though Miriam Lane had told him all,
Because things seen are mightier than things heard,
Staggered and shook, holding the branch, and feared
To send abroad a shrill and terrible cry
Which in one moment like the blast of doom,
Would shatter all the happiness of the hearth,
Ann thus he passed and died unknown to all save
Miriam Lane."

Whom he made promise never to divulge until she saw him dead.

The similarity stops not here. We find even an expression analagous. Philip bears a life-long hunger in his heart. In Homeward Bound "the hungry longing" left me.

In a beautiful little poem, called "Links with Heaven," Miss Proctor has given us sentiments and ideas which betray a sympathy with the innate feelings, that are difficult to conceive in one who could write only from the experience of another. We are inclined to ask with wonder, from what hidden source has that knowledge been obtained, which enables her thus powerfully to pierce the deepest chords within a mother's heart? From her maternal tribulation she raises her to a contemplation of her dear one, safely sheltered in the arms of Jesus. She inspires her with a lofty ambition to be worthy of her little child, whose sublime destiny, now accomplished, she regards only as a disenthralled, beatified spirit. She bids her listen to its sweet, silver tones as they mingle in the choir of angels; and from the picture linned so faithfully to satisfy the mother yearning, she rises strong in fortifying grace to bear the will of heaven, even though it decree the rupture of her dearest household ties. But I will attempt no longer a description so faint and imperfect, but give my readers an opportunity of judging for themselves:

LINKS WITH HEAVEN.

Our God in Heaven, from that holy place,
   To each of us an angel guide has given;
But mothers of dead children have more grace—
   For they give angels to their God and Heaven.

How can a mother's heart feel cold or weary,
   Knowing her dearer self safe, happy, warm?
How can she feel her road too dark or dreary,
   Who knows her treasure sheltered from the storm?

How can she sin? our hearts may be unheeding,
   Our God forgot, our holy saints defied;
But can a mother hear her dead child pleading,
   And thrust those little angel hands aside?

Those little hands stretched down to draw her ever
    Nearer to God by mother love:—we all
Are blind and weak, yet surely she can never,
    With such a stake in heaven, fail or fall.

She knows that when the mighty angels raise
    Chorus in Heaven, one little silver tone
Is hers forever, that one little praise,
    One little happy voice, is all her own.

We may not see her sacred crown of honor,
    But all the angels flitting to and fro,
Pause, smiling as they pass,—they look upon her
    As mother of an angel whom they know.

One whom they left nestled at Mary's feet,—
    The children's place in Heaven;—who softly sings
A little chant to please them, slow and sweet,
    Or smiling, strokes their little folded wings;

Or gives them Her white lilies or Her beads
    To play with:—yet, in spite of flower or song,

They often lift a wistful look that pleads
  And asks Her why their mother stays so long.

Then our dear Queen makes answer, she will call
  Her very soon; meanwhile they are beguiled
To wait and listen while She tells them all—
  A story of Her Jesus as a child.

Ah! saints in Heaven may pray with earnest will,
  And pity for their weak and erring brothers;
Yet there is prayer in Heaven more tender still,—
  The little children pleading for their mothers.

Already we have observed that deep
underlying religious sentiment which per-
vades almost every emanation from Miss
Proctor's pen. Let her mood be ever so
joyous, her vein ever so cheerful, she never
descends to frivolity. Living as she did,
in strict conformity to the faith of her

deepest and most fervent convictions, she experiences a sweet contentment—a calm submission among the many checkered scenes she delineates. Her tone is always healthy; if she describes a sorrow, she finds a consolation. Never morbid, while admit-ting the ills of life, she often proves them a very necessity to a fuller realization of happiness. Her sympathies are never bar-ren, and in this lies the secret of her suc-cess. She indeed was no theorist; by the bed-side of the poor and desolate she learn-ed their woes and their afflictions. She could relinquish hours of social enjoyment to pass them in the haunts of poverty, alleviating by her presence, as well as by her purse, the hard condition of those whom Jesus has called to suffer like unto himself. Without this intimate acquaint-

ance, with scenes described, could she ever
have penned the following :

"THE CRADLE SONG OF THE POOR."

Hush ! I cannot bear to see thee
  Stretch thy tiny hands in vain;
Dear, I have no bread to give thee,
  Nothing, child, to ease thy pain !
When God sent thee first to bless me
  Proud and thankful too was I;
Now, my darling, I, thy mother,
  Almost long to see thee die.
Sleep, my darling, thou art weary;
God is good, but life is dreary.

I have watched thy beauty fading,
  And thy strength sink day by day,
Soon I know will want and fever,
  Take thy little life away.
Famine makes thy father reckless,
  Hope has left both him and me;

We could suffer all, my baby,
　　Had we but a crust for thee.
Sleep, my darling, thou art weary;
God is good, but life is dreary.

Better thou shouldst perish early,
　　Starve so soon, my darling one,
Than in helpless sin and sorrow
　　Vainly live as I have done.
Better that thy angel spirit,
　　With my joy, my peace, were flown,
Than thy heart grow cold and careless,
　　Reckless, hopeless, like my own.
Sleep, my darling; thou art weary;
God is good, but life is dreary.

I am wasted, dear, with hunger,
　　And my brain is all opprest,
I have scarcely strength to press thee,
　　Wan and feeble, to my breast.
Patience, baby, God will help us,
　　Death will come to thee and me,

He will take us to His Heaven,
  Where no want or pain can be.
Sleep, my darling, thou art weary;
God is good, but life is dreary.

Such the plaint that, late and early,
  Did we listen, we might hear
Close beside us,—but the thunder
  Of a city dulls our ear.
Every heart, as God's bright angel,
  Can bid one such sorrow cease;
God has glory when his children
  Bring his poor ones joy and peace!
Listen! nearer, while she sings,
Sounds the fluttering of wings!

In the autumn of 1860, the idea was conceived by the Rev. Dr. Gilbert of opening a night refuge in his parish. This great charity won the entire sympathy of Miss Proctor. She published, for the benefit of this much needed institution, a collection of her religious and other poems. She appeals to the public in her preface most touchingly:

"A shelter through the bleak winter nights—leave to rest in some poor shed—instead of wandering through the pitiless streets, is a boon we could hardly deny to a starving dog; and yet we have all known that in this country, in this town, many of our miserable fellow-creatures were pacing the streets through the long weary nights, without a roof to shelter them, without food to eat, with their poor rags soaked in rain, and only the bitter winds of Heaven for companions; women and children utterly forlorn and helpless, either wandering about all night or crouching under a miserable archway, or, worst of all, seeking in death or sin the refuge denied them elsewhere. It is a marvel that we could sleep in peace in our warm, comfortable homes with this horror at our very door."

After describing quite minutely the rules of the institution, which are conceived in the widest spirit of charity, she concludes as follows:

"We all meditate long and often on the many kinds of sufferings borne for us by our Blessed Redeemer; but, perhaps, if we consider a moment, we shall most of us confess that the one we think of least often—the one we compassionate least of all—is the only one of which he deigned to tell us himself, and for which he himself appealed to our pity in the Divine complaint,—'the foxes have holes, and the birds of the air have nests, but the Son. of Man has not where to lay His head.'"

From the publication above referred to but two poems are selected, from the very fact that each alike possesses the claim of intrinsic beauty and merit. A Pagan aphorism says : "Those whom the Gods love, die young." Christian experience is the same; how often our dear Lord calls, in their extreme youth, the beautiful, the gifted, the sunlight of our homes, they who have been with us so short a time, and yet have left a life-long record. Miss Proctor was surely one of these; long and tenderly will she be mourned by her many friends and admirers, while in heart-felt sorrow they deplore the void occasioned by her early death.

THE ANGEL'S BIDDING.

Not a sound is heard in the Convent—
  The Vesper Chant is sung,
The sick have all been tended,
The poor nun's toils are ended
  Till the Matin bell has rung.
All is still, save the clock that is ticking
  So loud in the frosty air,
And the soft snow falling as gently
  As an answer to a prayer.

But an angel whispers, "O sister,
  You must rise from your bed to pray—
In the silent deserted chapel,
  You must kneel till the dawn of day;

For, far on the desolate moorland,
  So dreary, and bleak, and white,
There is one, all alone and helpless,
  In peril of death to-night.

"No sound on the moorland to guide him,
  No star in the murky air;
And he thinks of his home and his loved ones
  With the tenderness of despair;
He has wandered for hours in the snow-drift,
  And he strives to stand in vain,
And so lies down to dream of his children,
  And never to rise again.

"Then kneel in the silent chapel
  Till the dawn of to-morrow's sun,
And ask of the Lord you worship
  For the life of that desolate one;
And the smiling eyes of his children
  Will gladden his heart again,
And the grateful tears of God's poor ones
  Will fall on your soul like rain!

"Yet leave him alone to perish,
  And the grace of your God implore,
With all the strength of your spirit,
  For one who needs it more.
Far away, in the gleaming city,
  Amid perfume, and song, and light,
A soul that Jesus has ransomed
  Is in peril of sin to-night.

"The temper is close beside him,
  And his danger is all forgot.
And the far-off voices of childhood
  Call aloud, but he hears them not;
He sayeth no prayer, and his mother—
  He thinks not of her to-day,
And he will not look up to Heaven,
  And his angel is turning away.

"Then pray for a soul in peril—
  A soul for which Jesus died;
Ask by the cross that bore Him,
  And by her who stood beside;

And the angels of God will thank you,
   And bend from their thrones of light,
To tell you that Heaven rejoices,
   At the deed you have done to-night."

OUR TITLES.

Are we not Nobles—we who trace
  Our pedigree so high,
That God, for us and for our race,
  Created Earth and Sky, -
And Light, and Air, and Time, and Space,
  To save us and then die?

Are we not Princes—we who stand
  As heirs beside the Throne;
We who can call the promised land
  Our Heritage, our own;
And answer to no less command,
  Than God's, and His alone?

Are we not Kings? both night and day,
  From early until late,

About our bed, about our way,
　A guard of Angels wait;
And so we watch, and work, and pray,
　In more than royal state.

Are we not holy? Do not start;
　It is God's sacred will,
To call us temples set apart,
　His Holy Ghost may fill
Our very food—O hush! my heart,
　Adore it-and be still !

Are we not more? our life shall be
　Immortal and divine,
The nature Mary gave to Thee,
　Dear Jesus, still is thine;
Adoring in thy heart I see
　Such blood as beats in mine.

O God, that we can dare to fail,
　And dare to say we must;
O God, that we can ever trail
　Such banners in the dust;

Can let such starry honors pale,
  And such a blazon rust!

Shall we upon such titles bring
  The taint of sin and shame?
Shall we the children of the King,
  Who hold so grand a claim,
Tarnish by any meaner thing
  The glory of our name?

IN MEMORIAM.

They are not dead—my darlings-
They meet me at the door,
The patter of their little feet
Is sounding from the floor.

The rustle of their garments soft,
The tones that murmuring fell,
In cadence sweet, upon my ear,
Forbid a last farewell.

Oh! many are the fancies
That still my heart beguile,
While reason sleeps, they enter,
And cheat my love the while.

Sometimes I am returning
  From a little absence—long
To the dear ones who are watching
  For their mother's safe return.

I see them far off, coming,
  And half I bend to meet;
The Welcome, soft and tender,
  That was ever mine to greet.

First of all, my darling Mary,
  With her bright and happy brow;
The sunlight of her beauty
  Is beaming on me now.

And by her side another,
  With his wealth of golden hair;
I can see his sunny ringlets
  Tossing wildly in the air.

Alas! It is but dreaming,
  My darlings are at rest;

But the mother-heart is yearning
 To fold them to her breast.

Oh! my heart is full of memories,
 Mine eyes are full of tears;
God only knows the anguish,
 'Mid the calmness which appears.

THE ANGEL OF MY WEARY HOUR.

TO SARAH MARIE.

An angel strayed from Eden's bowers,
　Nor found again its home so dear;
For wandering near this world of ours,
　With trembling wing and heart of fear—

It chanced upon our parent cot,
　At the sweet hour of eventide;
Our little ones—a circle sweet—
　Were gathered to the mother side.

With raised eyes and clasped hands,
　Their hearts went in one choral strain,
Oh! God protect our father dear,
　And bring him safely back again.

7

Then as that prayer of love went up,
  Like incense on the floating air,
The angel downward bent his wing,
  And found a home amid them there.

Now closely folded to my breast,
  From morn till evening's dewy hour,
I clasp this solace, warm and close,
  The angel of my weary hour.

THE BEAUTIFUL.

The beautiful is round us, where'er we chance to stray,
By nature's silvery fountain, where its gleaming waters
    play;
In the rustling of the forest leaf, in the flower lips of
    the sod,
In all the speech-like eloquence that telleth us of God.

The beautiful is round us in the morning's early beam,
When it lifts the shadowy mantle from the hill-tops lone
    and green;
And when the night unfoldeth its glories to our view,
The beautiful comes mingled with the infinite and true.

In the spring-time's early breath, in the summer's fer-
    vid beam,
In the dancing of the zephyrs, the sparkle on the
    stream,

In the russet robe of autumn, its crimson and its gold,
In the jewels icy winter hangs on her forehead old.

The beautiful, the beautiful comes with its promptings
    pure,
And telleth us of glories which ever shall endure;
For it whispers, as it passes, earth's brightest trea-
    sure known
Is but a shadow faint and weak from God's celestial
    throne.

THE OLD COTTAGE.

DEDICATED TO L. K.

———

Beneath the ancient roof-tree, beneath these lowly walls,
What recollections of the past my memory recalls;
The bounding step of childhood, its wild and merry
    glee,
The sobered tread of manhood, all found a home in
    thee

The holy joy of motherhood, the pang of parting breath,
The farewell sad, the meeting fond, and the bitter wail
    of death,
Have each been felt and known here, in days now past
    and gone;
But their memory is recorded in the old hearth stone.

Oh! many a fervid blessing from mother's lips were
    shed,
As heart to heart in fervent love the dear good night
    was said;
Those lingering voices of the past once in this quaint
    old room
Discoursed their tones of joyful love, a soul-dispelling
    gloom.

In other homes we find them, this once dear household
    band,
While she, the fond and loving, "a mother in the land,"
Renews the love of olden time as every added face
Bespeaks a well-accorded claim, the children of her
    race.

Then sacred be the memories of this old cottage home,
Her sons will not forget them, though distant far they
    roam;
For when the soul grows weary with the changeful and
    the new,
Here shall they find those golden links, the faithful and
    the true.

TO J. C. G.

—

I know you in your half disguise,
  And J. C. G. will ever blend
With those dear memories of the past
  That bind me to my absent friend.

I greet you with my pen and ink,
  And say a loving "How d'ye do?"
And wish that you with me could look
  Upon the Sound so clear and blue.

The white sails o'er the waters bend,
  The swallows skim along the sea;
The air is trembling with the sound
  Of nature's gushing melody.

Familiar grown, the robins come
    To pick the crumbs close by the door,
Then with their trilling roundelay
    They thank us for the daily store.

'Mid scenes like these the heart grows young,
    Renews its youth from nature's spring,
Nor craves one other wish beyond
    The simple pleasures which she brings.

A poet* that I like to con,
    Who in his day won much renown,
Proclaimed aloud the simple truth:
    "God made the country—man the town."

Here come the children from the woods,
    (The angel band you used to say,)
Whose kindling smiles and merry moods
    Could fill your heart with love alway.

With their return, I say farewell!
    My busy pen can chat no more;
I must away, but ere I go,
    Believe me, yours for ever more.

*Cowper.

SILVER LAKE—RYE.

Silver Lake, in thy calm beauty,
  Dewy twilight spreads her glow;
Crimson tipped, her pencil lingers
  For the moon's effulgent flow.

In thy depths and on thy bosom
  Softened shadows sweetly lie,
Circling shore, fair verdant islets,
  And the Heaven-reflected sky.

On thy waves, in sportive beauty,
  Sails the swan in queenly pride,
Dipping now her graceful plumage,
  Breasting then a rushing tide.

Deeper, duskier grow the shadows,
  Limned against the evening sky;
Dome-like towers and slender spires
  Seem to meet the charmed eye.

While our boat is swiftly gliding
  O'er the waters soft and clear,
Music, with its softened cadence,
  Floats upon the listening ear.

By the silver chime of waters,
  We are near the quaint old mill;
While I tell you of its story,
  Let our boat float at its will.

Years ago, perchance one hundred,
  Three men, crippled, so they say,
Built these sides, so old and hoary,
  Which you look on every day.

But the autumn mists are falling,
  And the moon is riding high,

Glimmering lights amid the foliage
  Tell me that our home is nigh.

So farewell! sweet lake of beauty,
  I would ever, ever glide
On thy pure, translucent bosom,
  With my dear ones at my side.

TO AN ABSENT CHILD.

———

"Good night! God bless you mamma!
　　Good night! my mamma dear!"
Those oft-repeated tender words
　　Still linger on my ear.

And for one moment I forget
　　My darling is away,
Nor heeds the mother longing
　　That fills my heart to-day.

How oft my book was laid aside,
　　My work flung from my knee,
While with a bounding step I flew,
　　At anxious call from thee.

Ah! then I learnt the pretext
  That brought me to your door,
As half in fear and all in love
  I heard the "one kiss more!"

You cannot know, my dear one,
  How deep this heart of mine,
With anxious hopes and tender fears,
  Responds the love of thine.

And often, very often,
  When sleep hath bowed your head,
I kneel in lonely vigil
  And pray beside your bed,

That you may be, not great but good—
  A higher, loftier aim,
As heavenly meed is better far
  Than earth's ephemeral fame.

Be gay, be happy, darling,
  But still where'er you roam,
Do not forget that spot, so sweet
  We call our cottage home.

EPITHALAMIUM.

A memory sweet for a fair young bride,
But what shall the offering be?
Shall it come from the golden mines of earth,
Or the depths of the sounding sea?

Shall its sheen be that of the ruby gleam,
Or the amethyst's paler hue?
Shall its light be that of the emerald beam,
Or the turquoise's softer blue.

Oh no! for already upon her brow
She weareth, in golden youth,
A crown that would pale all lesser ones—
'Tis woven of love and truth.

Then take from my heart, oh, gentle bride,
  A hope and a trusting prayer,
That sunbeams ever upon thy way
  Their golden hues may wear.

And still, as now, may bliss be thine,
  While days glide sweetly on,
With memories dear of a happy past,
  And hope in the yet to come.

ELIZABETH BARRETT BROWNING.

———

ELIZABETH BARRETT BROWNING is conceded
to be the poetess of our age. The preco·
cious pupil of her learned and distinguished father, she translated, at an in-
credibly early age, the grand old Greek,
and Latin masters, wrote poetry at ten,
more than well at fifteen. Miss Mitford,
in her extreme old age, thought nothing
of riding forty-five miles, and returning in
the evening of the same day, simply for
the pleasure which her friendship gave
her. She describes her at the age of six-

teen, as follows :—" She was the most interesting person I had ever seen, of a
slight, delicate figure, with a shower of
delicate curls falling on either side of a
most expressive face, large tender eyes,
richly fringed by dark eye-lashes, a smile
like a sunbeam, and such a look of youth-
fulness that I could scarcely persuade a
friend who saw her at this period that she
was the translatress of the 'Prometheus of
Æschylus,' the authoress of the 'Essay
on Mind.'" Her writings are frequently
marked with an intense feeling of humanity
and of womanhood, but not until the sorrow of her life fell upon her, not until
those sad, deep fountains of her heart
were stirred by the weight of a stun-
ning blow, do we observe that hue of
thought and feeling, especially that devo-

8

tional feeling, which characterized her later works. This sad event, which nearly killed Elizabeth Barrett, was the sudden and untimely death of her beloved brother. Her health was rendered. precarious by the bursting of a blood vessel, and the physicians ordered her, on the approach of winter, to a milder climate. Thither, accompanied by this dear and devoted relative, she departed. She derived much benefit from the change, until one fine summer morning he, accompanied by a few friends, left her for a pleasure excursion of some hours. By an accident the boat upset, and all on board perished — even their bodies were never found. It was not until the following year she could be removed to her home, so utterly prostrated was she by the horror of this bereavement. Then

the sole diversion of her thoughts was intellectual pursuits. Here she studied and
wrought, and found her consolation either
in the flowery walks of literature or the
rugged paths of science. Imagine this
delicate woman confined to one large and
darkened chamber for hours in every day,
reading books in almost every language
worth reading, giving her heart and soul
to those occupations which seemed to have
become the very aliment of her existence.
It has sometimes been regretted that her
theology, which was of a peculiar character, should have infused itself so largely
into her works ; and it is very remarkable
that with her profound scholarship, lofty
spirit, and often noble appreciation of the
great and good of past ages, she should
have permitted herself to give utterance

to expressions and sentiments that not only grate harshly on the feelings of many, but are in themselves as illiberal as falsely conceived. Unfortunately, in this respect, she is no exception to the generality of writers. But from the wide range of matter which is indubitably her own, we can select sufficient to enable us to leave out what would give neither pleasure nor profit. Almost through her entire works we miss the exquisite tenderness, the childlike play of emotion, that is so beautiful a concomitant of poetry. Her way to the heart seems so cold and stately, her sentences so profound, nature is overlayed, as it were, by the process, and while we wonder at her erudition, our sympathies are uninfluenced by her cold but correct process of reasoning. But there are times

when her heart can speak its grief in tones
of winning tenderness. Witness the prayer
in "Isobel's Child," how the mother speaks
in every word. Her pleadings are irresistible:

> " Oh! take not, Lord, my child away,
> Oh! take not to thy songful Heaven,
> The pretty babe that thou hast given,
> Or ere that I have seen him play,
> Around his father's knees, and known
> That he knew how my love has gone
> From all the world to him:
> Think, God, among the cherubin,
> How I shall shiver every day
> In thy pure sunshine, knowing where
> The grave-grass keeps it from his fair,
> Still cheeks, and feet at every tread
> His little body which is dead,
> And hidden in the turfy fold,
> Doth make thy whole warm earth a-cold.

O God, I am so young, so young,
I am not used to tears at nights
Instead of slumber, nor to prayer
With sobering lips and heart outwrung;
Thou knowest all my prayings were—
I bless thee, God, for past delights:
Thank God, I am not used to bear
Hard thoughts of death; the earth doth cover
No face from me of friend and lover,
And must the first who teaches me
The form of shrouds and funerals be
Mine own first-born beloved? he
Who taught me first this mother-love.
Dear Lord who spreadeth out above
Thy loving transpierced hands to meet,
All lifted, hearts with blessings sweet,
Pierce not my heart, my tender heart,
Thou madest tender. Thou who art
So happy in thy heaven alway,
Take not mine only bliss away."

Could anything reveal more perfectly the struggle of a mother's heart? and yet the prayer is enhanced by the beauty of the calm resignation which concludes the picture:

> "I changed the cruel prayer I made,
> And bowed my meekened face and prayed
> That God would do His will; and thus
> He did it nurse. He parted us,
> And his sun shows victorious
> The dead calm, and I am calm;
> And heaven is hearkening a new psalm."

This exquisite poem would seem to refute the idea that her way to the heart was circuitous; but like all children of genius she had her meteoric flashes, her dazzling gleams, though her bent seemed philosophical, satirical, nay, even political.

Her facility as a writer is wonderfully proved in the shortness of time in which was put into form her "Lady Geraldine's Court-ship." It is certainly one of the most charming love stories of any language—contains one hundred and three stanzas, and was written in twelve hours. Surely it must have been lying in her head and heart, says Miss Mitford. Mrs. Browning's biographers delight in a little incident connected therewith. They say her allusion to a poem of Browning's led to an introduction, and marriage followed soon. after. Let this be as it will, never was a union more replete with happiness. Hilliard, in his "Six Months in Italy," says a more perfect bliss is difficult to imagine, and this completeness arises not only from the rare qualities which each possesses, but from their perfect adaptation to each other. As he is full of manly power, so she is a type of the most delicate and sensitive womanhood. I have never seen a human frame which seemed so nearly a transcript of a celestial and immortal spirit. She is a soul of fire inclosed in a shell of pearl, nor is she more remarkable for genius and learning, than for her gentleness and docility of character. It is a privilege to know such beings singly and separately, but to see their powers quickened and their happiness rounded by the sacred tie of marriage is a cause for peculiar and lasting gratitude. A union so complete as theirs, in which the mind has nothing to crave, nor the heart to sigh for, is cordial to behold and soothing to remember. In her sonnets from the Portugese, which might have been called *leaves from her own heart*, she writes thus on love:

> " Yes, love, mere love, is beautiful indeed,
> And worthy of acceptation. Fire is bright,
> Let temple.burn or flax, an equal light
> Leaps in the flame from cedar plant or weed,
> And love is fire and when I say it, need
> I love thee? Mark; I love thee! in thy sight
> I stand transfigured, glorified aught
> With conscience of the sun-rays that proceed
> Out of my face toward thine. There's nothing low
> In love, when love the lowest, meanest creatures
> Who love God, God accepts while loving so,
> And what I feel across the inferior features
> Of what I am doth flash itself, and show
> How that great work of love enhances nature's."

The graceful pen of the gifted Tucker-
man was the first American who gave to
Mrs. Browning her just meed of praise.
While he does justice to her genius, he

shrinks not from her faults, but with a discrimination and honesty which is the charm of a biogropher, he presents her fairly and impartially to the reader. He says she is often Dantesque and Miltonic. As an evidence, the following. Lucifer narrates an incident in the drama of Adam and Eve:

"Dost thou remember, Adam, when the curse
Took us from Eden. On a mountain peak,
Half sheathed in prismal woods, and glittering
In spasms of awful sunshine at that hour,
A lion crouched—part raised from his paws,
With his calm, massive face turned full on thine,
And his mane listening. When the ended curse
Left silence to the world right suddenly,
He sprang up rampant and stood straight and stiff,
As if the new reality of death were dashed against his
        eyes,
And roared so fierce—such thick, carniverous passion in
        his throat,

Tearing a passage through the wrath and fear,
And roared so wild, and smote from all the hills
Such fast, keen echoes, crumbling down the oaks
To distant silence, that the forest beasts,
One after one, did mutter a response
In savage and in sorrowful complaint,
Which trailed along the gorges. Then at once
He fell back and rolled crashing from the height,
Hid by the dark-orbed pines."

As an evidence of versatility of talent, read the following, taken from "Aurora Leigh:"

"By the way, the works of women are symbolical,
We sew, sew, prick our fingers, dull our sight,
Producing what? A pair of slippers, sir,
To put on when you're weary; or a stool
To tumble over and vex you— * * *
Or else, at best, a cushion where you lean
And sleep, and dream of something we are not,
But would be for your sake."

She makes Romney Leigh criticise her works, and give us a specimen of satire:

'Oh excellent! what grace! what facile turns!
What fluent sweeps! what delicate discernment—
Almost thought! The book does honor to the sex
We hold. Among our female writers we make room
For this fair author, and congratulate the country
That produces, in these times, such women competent
To *spell.*

Another possesses a bitterness almost un-exampled:

                    I perceive
The headache is too noble for my sex.
You think the heartache would sound decenter,
Since that's the woman's special, proper ache,
And altogether tolerable—except
To a woman.

What a volume of hopes and fears are conveyed in the following expressions:

My Father—Thou hast knowledge,
Only Thou. How dreary 'tis for women t sit still
On winter nights, by solitary fires,
And hear the nations praising them far off.

   To have our books
Appraised by love associated with love,
While we sit loveless; it is hard, you think?
At least, 'tis mournful. Fame, indeed, 'twas said,
Means simply love. *It was a man said that.*

Happy for her, the song teachings of her muse found a blissful experience in the practical relations of life. I feel constrained to prove this by the words of Robert Browning to his wife, in his poem entitled "One Word More:"

"God be thanked, the meanest of his creatures
Boasts two souls sides—one to face the world with,
One to show a woman when he loves her.
"This to you—yourself, my moon of poets.
Ah, but that's the world side—there's the wonder;
Thus they see you, praise you, think they know you.
There in turn I stand with them and praise you
Out of my own self. I dare to phrase it,
But the best is when I glide from out them,
Cross a step or two of dubious twilight.
Come out on the other side. The novel
Silver, silent lights and darks undreamed of,
Where I hush and bless myself with silence."

Immediately after their marriage the Brownings removed to Italy. This became their permanent home. It has been asked by one of her biographers, might not the poetic bays of the laureate of England have been disputed if they had remained there? It is now a fact uncontroverted that no writers since the days of Shakspeare have written finer poetry than that which is now under consideration.   Mrs. Browning always doubted her own originality. She had a perfect scorn for her earlier productions, and yet her power over language was so wonderful, so enlarged, so varied, she possessed such a vocabulary for her own choice, that she at least was independent of all others.   With a skill peculiarly her own, she knew how to select those which give a charm to the idea and beauty to the imagery—a strength to the whole.   "Words are instruments of music."   Who can fail to observe this in the Iliad of Homer, and the poems of Walter Scott?   You can almost hear the tramp of the steed, the clash of the steel, the rush of the hosts, the onset, the clamor, the din; and this not by the power of the idea more than the words which clothe it.

Some of Mrs. Browning's translations from the Greek Christian poets are very fine. The following is from " John of Damascene," she says herself, the tears seem to trickle audibly:

"From my lips in their defilement,
From my heart in its beguilement,
From my tongue which speaks not fair,
From my soul, stained everywhere,
O, my Jesus, take my prayer.

I have sinned· more than she,
Who learning where to meet with Thee,
Aud bringing myrrh the highest priced,
Anointed bravely, from her knee,
Thy blessed feet accordingly,
My God, my Lord, my Christ,

> As Thou saidst not depart
> To that suppliant from her heart,
> Scorn me not, O Word that art
> The gentlest Words of all words said,
> But give Thy feet to me instead,
> That tenderly I may them kiss,
> And clasp them close and never miss,
> With overdropp'ng tears, as free
> And precious as that myrrh could be,
> T' anoint Thee bravely from my knee,
> Wash them with my tears."

Who can say one word to this wail of a contrite heart? Our hearts bow to the anguish depicted, and yield their simple, silent tribute of acknowledgment. She speaks thus of St. Gregory of Nazianzen:— "A noble and tender man was this Gregory, and so tender because so noble, a man to lose no cubit of his stature for being looked at

steadfastly or struck at reproachfully. You
may cast me down, he said, from my Bishop's
throne, but you cannot banish me from before God's. And Bishop he was, his saintly
crown stood higher than his tiara, and his
loving martyr-smile, the crown of a nature
more benign than his fortune, shone up
toward both. The desire of his soul being
for solitude, quietude and that silent religion
which should rather 'be than seem.' But
his father's head bent whitely before him,
even in the chamber of his brother's death,
and Basil, his beloved friend, the 'half of
his soul,' pressed on him with the weight of
love, and Gregory feeling their tears upon
his cheeks did not count his own, but took
up the priestly office. Little did he care
for Bishoprics or high places of any kind,
but he yielded. His student days at Athens,

where he and Basil read together poems
and philosophies, and holier things, were
the happiest of his life. He says of himself:
'As many stones were thrown at me as
other men had flowers,' nor was persecution
the worst evil,. for friend after friend, beloved after beloved, passed away from before his face, and the voice which charmed
them living spoke brokenly beside their
graves, his funeral orations marked sever-
ally the wounds of his heart. The follow·
ing extract is a wail of grief:

Where are my winged words? Dissolved in air.
Where is my flower of youth? All withered. Where
My glory? Vanished. Where the strength I knew
From comely limbs? Disease hath changed it too,
And bent.them. Where the riches and the lands?
God hath them, yea and sinner's snatching hands
Have grudged the rest. Where is my father, mother,

And where my blessed sister, my sweet brother?
Gone to the grave! There did remain for me
Alone my Fatherland, till destiny,
Malignly stirring a black tempest, drove
My foot from that last rest. And now I rove
Estranged and desolate a foreign shore,
And drag my mournful life and age all o'er
Throneless and cityless, and childless, save
This father-care for children which I have,
Living from day to day on wandering feet.
Where shall I cast this body? What will greet
My sorrows with an end? What gentle ground
And hospitable grave will wrap me round?
Who last my dying eyelids stoop to close?
Some saint, the Saviour's friend, or one of those
Who do not know him. The air interpose
And scatter these words too.

In the Cry of the Children, Mrs. Browning expresses her intense sympathy with the woes of the desolate and the unfortu-

nate; it has been called a twin poem with
"Hood's Song of the Shirt." How feelingly
she pleads their sufferings—the blank hope-
lessness of their condition. The opening is
particularly fine.

"Do you question the young children in their sorrow,
  Why their tears are falling so?
The old man may weep for his to-morrow,
  Which is lost in long ago;
The old tree is leafless in the forest,
  The old year is ending in the frost,
The old wound, if stricken, is the sorest,
  The old hope is hardest to be lost;
But the young, young children, O my brothers,
  Do you ask them why they stand
Weeping sore before the bosoms of their mothers,
  In our happy Fatherland.

" They look up with their pale and sunken faces,
  And their looks are sad to see,

For the man's hoary anguish draws and presses
  Down the cheeks of infancy.
'Your old earth,' they say, ' is very dreary;
  Our young feet,' they say, ' are very weak ;
Few paces have we taken, yet are weary
  Our grave-rest is very far to seek.'
Ask the aged why they weep, and not the children :
  For the outside earth is cold;
And we young ones stand without, in our bewildering,
  And the graves are for the old."

Remarkable for its beautiful figures and
sweet fancies, is the following extract taken
from

THE POET'S VOW:

"Eve is a two-fold mystery,
    The stillness earth doth keep,
The motion wherewith human hearts
    Do each to either leap;

As if all souls between the poles
　Felt parting comes in sleep.

The rowers lift their oars to view
　Each other in the sea;
The landsmen watch the rocking boats
　In a pleasant company;
While up the hill go gladlier still
　Dear friends by two and three

"The peasant's wife hath looked without
　Her cottage door and smiled,
For there the peasant drops his spade
　To clasp his younngest child;
Which hath no speech, but its hands can reach,
　And stroke his forehead mild."

The following poem illustrates a remark
ably fine conception of the tender loving
ness of the Great Creator. The conclud·
ing verse is remarkably touching:

"HE GIVETH HIS BELOVED SLEEP."

" Of all the thoughts of God that are
.Borne inward unto souls afar,
Along the Psalmist's music deep,
Now tell me if that any is
For gift or grace, surpassing this—
'He giveth His beloved sleep.'

What would we give to our beloved,
The hero's heart to be unmoved,
The poet's star-tuned harp to sweep,
The patriot's voice to teach and rouse
The monarch's crown to light the brows?
He giveth his beloved sleep.

" What do we give to our beloved?
A little faith all undisproved,
A little dust to overweep;
And bitter memories to make
The whole earth blasted for our sake.
He giveth His beloved sleep.

"'Sleep soft, beloved!' we sometimes say,
But have no tune to charm away
Sad dreams that through the eyelids creep,
But never doleful dream again
Shall break the happy slumber when
He giveth His beloved sleep.

"O earth, so full of dreary noises,
O men, with wailing in your voices,
O delved gold, the wailer's heap,
O strife, O curse, that o'er it fall!
God strikes a silence through you all,
And Giveth his beloved sleep.

"His dews drop mutely on the hill,
His cloud above it saileth still,
Though on its slope men sow and reap,
More softly than the dew is shed,
Or cloud is floated overhead,
He giveth His beloved sleep.

"Aye men may wonder while they scan
A living, thinking, feeling man
Confirmed in such a rest to keep;
But angels say and through the word
I think their happy smile is heard—
He giveth his beloved sleep.

"For me my heart that erst did go
Most like a tired child at a show,
That sees through tears the mummers leap,
Would now its wearied vision close,
Would child-like on His love repose,
Who giveth his beloved sleep.

"And friends, dear friends, when it shall be
That this low breath is gone from me,
And round my bier ye come to weep,
Let one most loving of you all,
Say 'not a tear must o'er her fall,'
He giveth His beloved sleep."

Theodore Tilton says the poem of the
"Virgin Mary and Child Jesus," has mani-

festly followed Milton's style. It is given
entire :

THE VIRGIN MARY TO THE CHILD JESUS.

"But see the Virgin blest,
Hath laid her babe to rest."

Milton's Hymn on the Nativity.

"Sleep, sleep mine holy one !
My flesh, my lord, what name I do not know,
A name that seemeth not too high or low,
Too far from me or heaven,
My Jesus *that* is blest, that word being given,
By the majestic angel, whose command
Was softly as a man's beseeching said,
When I and all the earth appeared to stand
In the great overflow
Of light celestial, from his wings and head,
Sleep, sleep my saving *One !*

"Perchance this sleep, that shutteth out the dreary
  Earth-sounds and motions, opens on thy soul;
High dreams on fire with God,
  High songs that make the pathway where they roll
More bright than stars do theirs: and visions new
Of Thine eternal nature's old abode.
    Suffer this mother's kiss,
    Best thing that earthly is,
To glide the music and the glory through,
Nor Narrow in thy dream the broad upliftings
    Of any seraph wing,
Thus Noiseless, thus sleep, sleep, my dreaming One.

"The slumber of His lips meseems to run
Through my lips to mine heart—to all its shiftings
Of sensual life—bringing contrariousness
In a great calm. I feel I could lie down,
As Moses did, and die—and then live most.
I am 'ware of you Heavenly Presences,
That stand with your peculiar light unlost,
Each forehead with a high thought for a crown,
Unsunned i' the sunshine! I am 'ware ye throw

No shade against the wall! how motionless
Ye round me with your living statuary,
While through your whiteness, in and outwardly,
Continual thoughts of God appear to go
Like light's soul in itself. I bear, I bear
To look upon the dropt lids of your eyes,
Though their external shining testifies
To that beatitude, within which were
Enough to blast an eagle at his sun,
I fall not on my sad, clay face before ye—
        I look on His. I know
My spirit which dilateth with the woe
        Of his mortality,
        May well contain your glory,
        Yea, drop your lids more low,
Ye are but fellow-worshippers with me!
Sleep, sleep my Worshipped One!

" We sate among the stalls at Bethlehem,
The dumb kine from their fodder turning them,
        Softened their horned faces
        To almost human gazes

Toward the newly born.
The simple shepherds from the star-lit brooks
       Brought visionary looks,
As yet in their astonished hearing rung
       The strange, sweet angel-tongue.
The magi of the East, in sandals worn,
       Knelt reverent, sweeping round,
With long, pale beards, their gifts upon the ground,
       The incense, myrrh and gold
These baby hands were impotent to hold.
So let all earthlies and celestials wait
       Upon thy royal state.
       Sleep, sleep my Kingly One!

"I am not proud—meek angels ye invest
New meeknesses to hear such utterance rest
On mortal's lips—I am not proud—not proud!
Albeit in my flesh God sent His Son,
Albeit over Him my head is bowed
As others bow before Him, still mine heart
Bows lower than their knees. O centuries
That roll in visions, your futurities

My future grave athwart—
Whose murmurs seem to reach me while I keep
      Watch o'er this sleep.
Say of me as the heavenly said—thou art
The blessedest of women!—blessedest,
Not holiest, not noblest—no high name,
Whose height misplaced may pierce me like a shame,
When I sit meek in Heaven!
                  For me, for me,
God knows that I am feeble like the rest!
I often wandered forth, more child than maiden,
Among the midnight hills of Galilee,
      Whose summits looked heaven laden,
Listening to silence as it seemed to be
God's voice, so soft, yet strong—so fair to press
Upon my heart as Heaven did on the height,
And waken up its shadows by a light,
And show its vileness by a holiness.
Then I knelt down, most silent like the night,
      Too self-renounced for fears,
Raising my small face to the boundless blue,
Whose stars did mix and tremble in my tears,
God heard them falling after—with the dew,

" So, seeing my corruption, can I see
This incorruptible now born of me,
This fair new innocence no sun did chance
To shine on, (for even Adam was no child,)
Created from my nature all defiled,
This mystery, from out mine ignorance,
Nor feel the blindness, stain, corruption, more
Than others do, or I did heretofore?
Can hands wherein such burden pure has been,
Not open with the cry 'unclean, unclean,'
More oft than else beneath the skies?
        Ah King, ah Christ, ah Son!
The kine, the shepherds, the abase'd wise,
        Must all less lowly wait
        Than I, upon Thy state,—
        Sleep, sleep my Kingly One!

Art Thou a King, then? Come, His universe
Come, crown me Him a King!
Pluck rays from all such stars as never fling
Their light where fell a curse,
And make a crowning for his kingly brow!

What is my word? Each empyreal star
    Sits in a sphere afar
    In shining ambuscade,
    The child-brow crowned by none,
    Keeps its unchildlike shade,
    Sleep, sleep my crownless One!

"Unchildlike shade!—No other babe doth wear
An aspect very sorrowful as thou.
No small babe smiles, my watching heart has seen
To float like speech the speechless lips between;
No dove-like cooing in the golden air,
No quick, short joys, leaping babyhood.
    Alas! our earthly good
In Heaven thought evil, seems too good for Thee,
    Yet sleep, my weary One!

And then the drear, sharp tongue of prophecy,
With the drear sense of things which shall be done,
Doth smite me inly, like a sword! a sword!
(That 'smites the shepherd,') then I think aloud
The words 'despised,'—'rejected,' every word

Recoiling into darkness as I view
    The darling on my knee.
Bright angels,—move not!—lest ye stir the cloud
Betwixt my soul and His futurity!
I must not die with mother's work to do,
    And could not live—and see.

    " It is enough to bear
    This image still and fair—
    This holier in sleep,
    Than a saint at prayer;
    This aspect of a child
    Who never sinned or smiled,
    This presence in an infant's face,
    This sadness most like love;
    This love than love more deep,
    This weakness like omnipotence,
    It is so strong to move.
    Awful is this watching place,
    Awful what I see from hence—
    A king, without regalia,

A God, without the thunder.
A child without the heart for play;
Aye, a Creator, rent asunder
From his first glory and cast away
On his own world, for me alone
To hold in hands created, crying—Son !

" That tear fell not on thee,
Beloved, yet thou stirrest in thy slumber !
Then stirring not for glad sounds out of number,
Which through the vibratory palm-trees runs
 From summer wind and bird,
 So quickly hast thou heard
 A tear fall silently ?—
 Wak'st thou, O loving One ? "

Sufficient poems and extracts have been given to render my readers familiar with the style of Mrs Browning, and yet they are almost as nothing to the vast store from which they are taken. Robert Browning, the happy partner of her too short married life, although possessing large claims to our consideration, is not equally known with his wife as connected with her, and out of justice to a fine poet, I quote some of the recollections of a celebrated English writer, who thus speaks of him :—" It was at the close of an entertainment, graced by Wordsworth, Landor, Talfourd and many other celebrities of the day, that the (then) young author of 'Paracelsus' was called upon to respond to the toast 'The Poets of England.' That he performed the task with grace and modesty, and that he looked still younger than he was, I well remember. And," she continues, "I never see his books nor read his plays without wishing that we had actors and a stage to represent them; his 'Blot on the Scutcheon,' ' Colombe's Birth-

day' and 'Lucia,' are evidences of his
dramatic ability." A little extract from the
'Englishman in Italy,' the same writer says,
appeared to her like a picture by Rubens,
pulpy, juicy, full of bright color and rich
in detail; to know that Ruskin thought it
remarkably fine is no mean praise."

But to-day not a boat reached Salerno,
     So back to a man
Came our friends, with whose help in the vineyards
     Grape-harvest began;
In the vat half way up on our house-side,
     Like blood the juice spins,
While your brother all bare-legged is dancing,
     Till breathless he grins;
Dead beaten in effort on effort,
     To keep the grapes under,
Since still when he seems all but master,
     In pours the fresh plunder

From girls who keep coming and going
   With basket on shoulder—

Meanwhile see the grape-bunch they've brought you,
   The rain-water slips
O'er the heavy blue bloom on each globe,
   Which the wasp on your lips
Still follows with fretful persistence—
   Nay, taste while awake,
This half of a curd-white smooth cheese-ball,
   That peals flake by flake
Like an onion's, each smoother and whiter;
   Next sip this weak wine
From the thin green flask with its stopper
   A leaf of the vine,
And end with the prickly pear's red flesh,
   That leaves through its juice
The stony black seeds on your pearl teeth—

And so on.

A poem of his, which is very popular

having the rather long title: " How they brought the good news from Ghent to Aix," contains life-like descriptions and exhibits the peculiar style of the writer. The first and last verses are here given:

I sprang to the stirrup, and Joies, and he,
I galloped, Dick galloped, we galloped all three,
Good speed! cried the watch as the gate-bolts undrew,
Speed! echoed the wall to us galloping through;
Behind shut the postern, the light sank to rest,
And into the midnight we galloped abreast.

Not a word to each other, we kept the great pace,
Neck by neck, stride by stride, never changing our place.
I turned in my saddle and made the girths tight,
Then shortened the stirrup and set the pique right, .
Rebuckled the check strap, chained slacker the bit,
Nor galloped less steadily, Roland, a whit.

*   *   *   *   *   *   *   *   *   *

Then I cast loose my buff-coat, each holster let fall,
Shook off both my jack-boots, let go belt and all,
Stood up in the stirrup, leaned, patted his ear,
Called my Ronald! his pet-name, my horse, without peer,
Clapped my hands, laughed and sang, any noise bad
    or good,
Till at length into Aix Roland galloped and stood.

And all I remember is friends flocking round,
As I sate with his head twixt my knees to the ground,
And no voice but was praising this Roland of mine,
As I poured down his throat our last measure of wine,
Which (the Burgesses voted by common consent,)
'Was no more than his due who brought good news
    from Ghent.

The compass of this little work admits of no more borrowings, or we might still go on to an infinitude; after all, a life is told chiefly in its beginning and its close. Mrs. Browning's then is told in these brief words: She was born in 1809, died June 29, 1861.

SONG.

TO KITTIE B.

———

Autumn winds are wailing,
Lone stars are paling,
Over the distant sea.

While my heart prayeth,
List what it sayeth,
Dearest to thee.

Child so loved and treasured,
Fondly and unmeasured,
Long, long may it be.

Golden each morrow,
Freed from all sorrow,
Guarded so tenderly.

Thus ever be thy way,
'Till God's supernal ray
Enfold thee eternally

NEW YEAR SONG OF 1867.

Tripping along, tripping along,
With tones of gladness and words of song,
A beautiful maid with dancing feet,
Hark to her words as she bends to greet
   A Happy New Year to All!

Shining amid her golden hair,
Are buds of promise and flowerets rare,
For each and all she has words of cheer,
Softly they fall on the listening ear—
   A Happy New Year to All!

From her sister lone, now stark and cold,
With a burthened year on her forehead old,

Quickly she turns on her mission away,
The time is pressing, she may not stay.

        A Happy New Year to All!

Tender I mingle in her refrain,
The wish of my heart again and again,
And oh! let me ask that your thoughts incline
To the same sweet wish for me and mine—

        A Happy New Year to All!

MARY THE IMMACULATE.

Oh holy Mary! mother mine,
    Here at thy feet my votive gifts I lay;
Inspire my soul, oh! nerve my trembling hand,
    A worthier offering of my heart to pay.

Angelic maiden! thou wert chosen
    Coeval with the ransom God decreed;
To angel lips thy sweet consent was given,
    And man was from his long probation freed.

Immaculate; no stain of sin might dwell,
    Within that shrine which God selected best;
Pure as the lily in its earliest dawn,
    That form of beauty where his son should rest.

Most lowly daughter of a kingly line,
  No eloquence inspired gushed from thy tongue;
No warblings from an unseen lyre,
  Floated thy sunny vales among.

Patient and humble, gentle and serene,
  Deep in thy heart each virtue found its rest;
Thy life was hidden in a lowly cot,
While God alone inspired thy holy breast.

Yet in the dimness of prophetic lore,
  Poets of old sang of that maiden pure,
Whose lofty mission and whose medium sweet,
  In humble greatness should for aye endure.

And to thy shrine, the child of genius comes,
  Basks in the sunshine of thy presence rare,
And while his canvass glows with added light,
  His soul invigorates itself in prayer.

Mother, sweet mother, previous to each call,
No child of sorrow ever pleads in vain;
Our Saviour God will not refuse the prayer
Of her, where on his infant head hath lain.

ECCE HOMO.

Behold the man in passive woe,
A willing victim at command;
Look at His meekly upturned face,
His streaming brow, His pinioned hands,—
The garment vile around Him thrown—
The sceptred reed—base mockery all!
Vainly ye gaze, insensate crowd!
From His pale lip no murmurs fall;
No plaint, no tone save words of love,
From that poor bruised and bleeding heart;
"Father, forgive this dire offence,
They know not yet their guilty part."
In memory of that love divine,
The Cross, the Thorn, the Sweat, the Spear,
Grant us to dwell within thy love—
And live in endless hope and fear.

ALFRED TENNYSON.

ALFRED TENNYSON impresses us as a man of genius, high and lofty in his conceptions, notwithstanding the many crudities and verbosities, which his warmest friends will not attempt to deny. It might be thought almost excusable for one who owes his high position to court favor, a certain bias or leaning to the eccentricities or foibles of the great, but it is scarcely to be found in all his works. He has discovered that virtue in lowly places which stamps its possessor noble—

> "A simple maiden in her flower
> Were worth a hundred coat of arms."

Is an eloquent exposition of his sentiments.
Again in the same poem :

> "Howe'er it be it seems to me
>   'Tis only noble to be good,
> Kind hearts are more than coronets,
>   And simple faith than Norman blood."

He inveighs against pride of birth also,
in "The Lord of Burleigh," where a simple
village maiden is wooed and won by one
whom she conceives to be of her own station, but who is "Lord of Burleigh, fair and
free." Wearied with stateliness, and pining,
for the simple lowliness of her former condition, she nevertheless

> "Shaped her heart with woman's meekness,
> To all duties of her rank,
> But a trouble weighed upon her,

And perplexed her night and morn,
With the burthen of an honor,
Unto which she was not born,
And she murmured, 'Oh that he
Were once more that landscape painter
Which did win my heart from me!'"

But his loyalty to merit alone is still more strictly defined in his exposition of a gentleman. What a manly independence breathes in every line. The true estimate of worth is not in the accidental gifts of wealth and power—it is discovered only in the gentle refinement—the high and manly principle of a well-ordered mind.

"The churl in spirit, up or down,
 Along the scale of ranks, through all
 To who may grasp a golden ball,
By blood a king, at heart a clown.

"The churl in spirit, howe'er he veil
   His want in forms for fashion's sake,
   Will let his coltish nature break
At seasons, through the gilded pale;

"For who can always act? but he
   To whom a thousand memories call,
   Not being less, but more than all,
The gentleness he seemed to be.

"So wore his outward best and joined
   ·Each office of the social hour
   To noble manners as the flower,
And native growth of noble mind.

"Nor ever narrowness or spite,
   Or villian fancy fleeting by,
   Drew in the expression of an eye,
When God in nature met in light.

"And thus he bore, without abuse,
   The grand old name of gentleman,
   Defamed by every charlatan
And soiled with all ignoble use."

Tennyson eulogizes a simple life, of which Wordsworth says: "That happy state when the heart luxuriates with indifferent things, wasting its kindliness on stocks and stones."

"Who makes it seem more sweet to be
   The little life of bank and brier,
   The bird that pipes his lone desire
And dies unheard within his tree.

"Than he that warbles long and loud,
   And drops at glory's temple gates,
   For whom the carrion vulture waits
To tear his heart before the crowd."

This little fragment gives one a fine idea of the appropriateness in which our poet clothes his thoughts. They come to us first in the expression of a simple description arrayed in russet robes, but when by comparison he gives us another view of humanity, we almost quail before the picture which he draws so fearfully vivid. If it be true that Tennyson is sometimes grotesque and occasionally morbid, may it not be forgiven to one who so often touches the lyre with such mastery of skill, and who will deny that even in his vagueness he has power to charm. We frequently .find a sentiment developed through the surroundings or atmosphere which he creates; and while his physical descriptions make us sensible of the outward world, they are but the pencil in the hand of the limner, marking the sadness, the desolation, or the joy and comfort which he designs to illustrate ; as an instance the following poem, which is given entire. Tuckerman says of it :—" These images, so full of graphic meaning, give us the lonely sensation that belongs to the deserted mansion ; and when at the close of each stanza the melancholy words of Mariana, bewailing her abandonment, fall on the ear with their sad cadence, we take in as completely the whole sense and sentiment, as if identified with it :"

MARIANA.

"With blackest moss the flower-plots
  Were thickly crusted, one and all;
The rusted nails fell from the knots
  That held the peach to the garden-wall ;

The broken sheds looked sad and strange;
  Uplifted was the clinking latch;
  Weeded and worn the ancient thatch
Upon the lonely, moated grange.
She only said, 'My life is dreary,
  He cometh not,' she said;
She said, 'I am aweary, aweary,
  I would that I were dead!'

" Her tears fell with the dews' at even;
  Her tears fell ere the dews were dried;
She could not look on the sweet Heaven,
  Either at morn or eventide.
After the flittering of the bats,
  When thickest dark did trance the sky,
  She drew her casement curtain by,
And glanced athwart the glooming flats,
She only said, 'The night is dreary,
  He cometh not,' she said;
She said, 'I am aweary, aweary,
  I would that I were dead!'

"Upon the middle of the night,
   Waking, she heard the night-fowl crow;
The cock sung out an hour ere light;
   From the dark fen the oxen's low
Came to her; without hope of change,
   In sleep she seemed to walk forlorn,
   Till cold winds broke the grey-eyed morn
About the lonely, moated grange.
She only said, 'The day is dreary,
   He cometh not,' she said;
She said, 'I am aweary, aweary,
   I would that I were dead!'

"About a stone-cast from the wall,
   A sluice with blackened waters slept,
And o'er it many, round and small,
   The clustered marish mosses crept.
Hard by a poplar shook alway,
   All silver green with gnarled bark,
   For leagues no other tree did mark
The level waste, the rounding grey.

She only said, 'My life is dreary,
  He cometh not,' she said;
She said, 'I am aweary, aweary,
  I would that I were dead!'

"And ever when the morn was low,
  And the shrill winds were up and away,
In the white curtain, to and fro,
  She saw the gusty shadow sway;
But when the moon was very low,
  And wild winds bound within their call,
  The shadow of the poplar fell
Upon her bed, across her brow.
She only said, 'The night is dreary,
  He cometh not,' she said;
She said, 'I am aweary, aweary,
  I would that I were dead!'

"All day within the dreamy house,
  The doors upon their hinges creaked;

The blue-fly sung i' the pane; the mouse
　　Behind the mouldering wainscot shrieked,
Or from the crevice peered about;
　　Old faces glimmered through the doors;
　　Old footsteps trod the upper floors;
Old voices called her from without.
She only said, 'My life is dreary,
　　He cometh not,' she said;
She said, 'I am aweary, aweary,
　　I would that I were dead!'

The sparrows chirrup on the roof,
　　The slow clock ticking, and the sound
Which to the wooing wind aloof
　　The poplar made, did all confound
Her sense; but most she loathed the hour
　　When the thick moated sunbeam lay
　　Athwart the chambers, and the day
Was sloping toward his western bower.
Then, said she, 'I am very dreary,
　　He will not come,' she said;

She wept, 'I am aweary, aweary,
   O God! that I were dead!'"

That Tennyson assimilates to the great
word painter, Crabbe, I quote from both as
proof, in his Day Dream he describes

"The butler with a flask
   Between his knees, half drained; and there
The wrinkled steward at his task;
   The maid of honor blooming fair;
The page has caught her hand in his;
   Her lips are severed as to speak;
His own are pouted to a kiss;
   The blush is fixed upon her cheek."

Crabbe paints a character thus:

"Fresh were his features, his attire was new,
Clean was his linen, and his jacket blue,
Of finest jean his trowsers tight and trim,
Brushed the large buckles at the silver rim."

The little extract which follows is as gossamer-like as if taken from the "Culprit Fay" itself:

"See what a lovely shell,
Small and pure as a pearl,
Lying close to my foot,
Frail, but a work divine,
Made so fairly well
With delicate spire and whorl,
How exquisitely minute,
A miracle of design?

"What is it? a learned man
Could give it a clumsy name.
Let him name it who can,
The beauty would be the same.

"The tiny cell is forlorn,
Void of the little living will
That made it stir on the shore.
Did he stand at the diamond door
Of his house in a rainbow frill?

Did he push, when he was uncurled,
A golden foot or a fairy horn,
Thro' his dim water-world?"

Tennyson's portraiture of a wife is perfect, if not too perfect for imitation:

"The intuitive decision of a bright
And thorough-edged intellect, to part
Error from crime; a precedence to withhold;
The laws of marriage charactered in gold,
Upon the blanched tablets of her heart,
A love still burning upward, giving light
To read those laws; an accent very low
In blandishment, but a most silver flow
    Of subtle faced counsel in distress,
Winning its way with extreme gentleness
Through all the outworks of suspicion's pride,
A courage to endure and to obey,
A hate of gossip, parlance, and of sway,
Crowned Isabel through all her placid life,
The queen of marriage, a most perfect wife."

In the trust reposed in Tennyson, we find the truest acknowledgment of his superiority. His characteristics are universal; sometimes "moving us through our deepest sympathies," he melts us with a kind of pleading love, as in "King Arthur" and "Guinevere." Again, in some grand truth, relating to human nature, he becomes Shaksperian:

"O purblind race of miserable men,
How many among us at this very hour
Do forge a life-long trouble for ourselves
By taking true for false, or false for true;
Here through the feeble twilight of this world
Groping, how many until we pass and reach
That other, where we see as we are seen."

And again where the "Lissome Vivien"

attemps to slander the blameless king, Merlin exclaims:

"O, my liege and king!
O, sinless man and stainless gentleman,
Who would'st against their own eye-witness fain
Have all men true and leal, all women pure;
How in the mouth of base interpreters,
From over-fineness not intelligible,
To things with every sense as false and foul
As the poached filth that floods the middle street,
Is thy white blamelessness accounted blame?"

The desertion of false friends in the hour
of need is portrayed in the same style
The prince Geraint encounters and vanishes
the wild count Limours. His followers,
seeing him stunned or dead, "rush on or
follow with the route behind:"

"But at the flash and motion of the man
They vanished panic-stricken, like a shoal
Of darting fish that on a summer morn
Adown the crystal docks at Camelot
Come slipping o'er the shadows on the sand,
But if a man who stands upon the brink
But lift a shining hand against the sun,
There is not left a twinkle of a fin
Betwixt the cressy islets white in flower;
So scared but at the motions of the man,
Fled all the boon companions of the earl,
And left him lying in the public way;
So vanish friendships only made in wine.

The descriptions that follow in this noble poem, one of "The Idyls of a king," are so fine, and many of them so applicable to the comparison above made, that it may be interesting to insert them. But

"Geraint being pricked
In combat with the followers of Limours
Bled underneath his armor secretly.
And Eniel heard the clashing of his fall,
Suddenly came and at his side all pale,
Dismounting, loosed the fastenings of his arms,
Nor let her true hand falter, nor blue eye
Moisten, till she had lighted on his wound,
And tearing off her veil of faded silk,
And bared her forehead to the blistering sun,
And swathed the hurt that drained her dear lord's
    life.
Then after all was done that hand could do
She rested, and her desolation came
Upon her, and she wept beside the way.

Now while she watched and prayed for
his swoon to pass, the huge and brutal earl
of Doorm

"Broad-faced with under face of russet beard,
Bound on a foray, rolling eyes of prey,

Came riding with a hundred lances up
But ere he came, like one that hails a ship,
Cried out with a big voice, "What, is he dead!"

.He commands Geraint to be carried to
his hall. The earl of Doorm

" Struck with a knife's haft hard against the board,
And called for flesh and wine to feed his spears.
And men brought in whole hogs and quarter beeves,
And all the hall was dim with steam of flesh;
And none spake a word, but all sat down at once,
And ate with tumult in the naked hall,
Feeding like horses, when you hear them feed.
" He spoke. the brawny spearman let his cheek
Bulge with the unswallowed piece, and turning,
    stared.'

Eniei scorns his proffered courtesies, and
maddened with his rage, he cries:

"I count it of no more avail,
Dame, to be gentle than ungentle with you;
Take my salute. Unknightly with flat hand,
However lightly smote her on the check. ·

"This heard Geraint, and grasping at his sword
(It lay beside him in the hollow shield.)
Made but a single bound, and with a sweep of it
Shore through the swarthy neck, and like a ball,
The russet-bearded head rolled on the floor."

Then in the confusion and the din of
men and women flying from before the face
of him, whom they accounted dead, Geraint
and Eniel passed from out that baleful
place:

"He mounted on a horse, reached a hand, and on
    his foot
She set her own and climbed; he turned his face
And kissed her climbing, and she cast her arms
About him, and at once they rode away."

If, as has been said, Tennyson nursed his muse at the pure fount of Shakspeare and of Dante, were it not wise to add the whole world of poesy was his mother, for in himself he so often seems to reproduce each different poet in his happiest mood. What follows is as strictly Homeric as if found in the pages of the Iliad:

>—"The new sun
> Beat through the blindless-casement of the room,
> And heated the strong warrior in his dreams,
> Who, moving, cast the coverlet aside,
> And bared the knoted column of his throat,
> The massive square of his heroic breast,
> And arms on which the standing muscle sloped,
> As slopes a wild brook o'er a little stone,
> Running too vehemently to break upon it."

Another:

"He dragged his eye-brow bushes down, and made
A snowy pent-house for his eyes."

Our own Bryant, in the full burst of his
gleeful heart, when escaping from the tur-
moil and drudgery of his outward active
life, he found himself reveling in the world
of nature, never uttered sentences more
deliciously sweet than the following:

"From the woods
Came voices of the well-contented doves;
The lark could scarce get out his notes for joy,
But shook his song together as he neared
His happy home, the ground. To left and right
The cuckoo told his name to all the hills;
The mellow owzel fluted in the elm;
The red-cap whistled; and the nightingale
Sang loud as though he were the bird of day."

This simple advocacy of the natural and the true must find admirers wherever the imagination of the heart is not vitiated by the unhealthy and flashy literature which, unfortunately for our day, is such a popular and current commodity. "It is calculated to cool the fevered blood and lead us to the fountains that go softly." This and more the simple and eloquent bard of " Rydal Mount" did in his day for English literature. This mysterious and wonderful flow of versification, when it takes simply the idiosyncracies of the poet, induces elements of expression peculiar to its possessor. This is particularly remarkable in Mrs. Browning and Tennyson. It is the quality which oftens earns for him the appellation of wordy. A cursory observer would almost be sure to pass this verdict. But will not the few extracts culled from a garden rich in poetic wealth, serve in part to refute the imputation. In the descriptions of the different styles of beauty there occurs a wonderful variety in the mode of delivery. "Eleanor, the beauty of thought;"

"Sometimes with most intensity
Gazing, I seem to see
Thought folded over thought, smiling asleep,
Slowly awakened, grow so large and deep
In thy large eyes that, overpowered quite,
I cannot veil or droop my sight,
But am as nothing in its light;
As though a star in inmost heaven set,
Even while we gaze on it,
Should slowly round the earth, and slowly grow,
To a full face, there like a sun remain
Fixed—then as slowly fade again,
And draw itself to what it was before;
So full, so deep, so slow,

Thought seems to come and go
In thy large eyes, imperial Eleanore."

　"Madeline, the ever varying:"

　"Frowns perfect-sweet along the brow
Light-glooming over eyes swim,
Like little clouds sun-fringed are thine,
　Ever varying Madeline.
Thy smiles and frowns are not aloof
　From one another—
Each to each is dearest brother;
Thus of the silken sheeny woof
Momently shot into each other,
　All the mystery is thine;
Smiling, frowning evermore,
Thou art perfect in love lore,
　Ever varying Madeline.

　"The sleeping beauty:

　"Year after year unto her feet,
　She lying on her couch alone,

Across the purple coverlet
  The maiden's jet black hair has grown.
On either side her tranced form
  Forth streaming from a braid of pearl;
The slumbrous light is rich and warm,
  And moves not on the rounded curl.

"She sleeps; her breathings are not heard,
  In palace chamber far apart,
The fragrant tresses are not stirred
  That lie upon her charmed heart;
She sleeps, nor dreams, but ever dwells
  A perfect form in perfect rest."

In the heart struggle depicted so glowingly
in the poem of "Love and Duty," there are
passages of tenderness and strength, hope
and despair, that one cannot read unmoved,
or without yielding his meed of admiration
and sympathy,

"Of love that never found its earthly close
What sequel? Streaming eyes and breaking hearts?
Or all the same as if it had not been?

" Will some one say, then why not ill for good?
Why took ye not your pastime? To that man
My work shall answer, since I knew the right?
And did it; for a man is not as God,
But then most Godlike being most a man.
So let me think 'tis well for thee and me—
Ill-fated that I am, what love is mine,
Whose foresight preaches peace, my heart so slow
To feel it. For how hard it seemed to me
When eyes love languid through half tears would
       dwell
One earnest, earnest moment upon mine,
                    All the wheels of time
Spun round in station, but the end had come.

" O then, like those who clench their nerves to
       rush
Upon this dissolution we two rose,

"There—closing like an individual life—
In one blind cry of passion and of pain,
Like bitter accusation even to death,
Caught up the whole of love and uttered it,
And bade adieu forever."

Some passages in the "Talking Oak," are very beautiful, he makes the old tree "garrulously given," speaks thus of Olivia, when Walter asks:

"If ever maid or spouse,
As fair as my Olivia, came
To rest beneath thy boughs."

After saying she is three times worth the all who flourished in times of hood and hoop, or while the patch was worn. He thus runs on:

"The day was warm,
At last, tired out with play,

She sank her head upon my arm,
   And at my feet she lay.

"Her eyelids dropped their silken eaves,
   I breathed upon her eyes,
Through all the summer of my leaves
   A welcome mixed with sighs.

"I took the swarming sound of life—
   The music from the town—
The whispers of the drum and fife,
   And lulled them in my own.

"Sometimes I let a sunbeam slip
   To light her shaded eye;
A second fluttered round her lip,
   Like a golden butterfly.

A third would glimmer on her neck,
   To make the necklace shine,
Another slid a sunny fleck,
   From head to ankle fine.

Then close and dark my arms I spread,
   And shadowed all her rest;
Dropt dews upon her golden head,
   An acorn in her breast.

The poem of "St. Agnes" gives us another distinct style of composition, and from all we know of the sweet saint, is a faithful portraiture:

ST. AGNES.

Deep on the convent roof the snows,
   Are sparkling to the moon;
My breath to Heaven like vapor goes,
   May my soul follow soon!
The shadows of the convent towers
   Slant down the snowy sward,
Still creeping with the creeping hours
   That lead me to my Lord·

Make Thou my spirit pure and clear
　　As are the frosty skies,
Or this first snow-drop of the year
　　That in my bosom lies.
As these white robes are soiled and dark,
　　To yonder shining ground,
As this pale taper's earthly spark,
　　To yonder argent round;
So shows my soul before the Lamb,
　　My spirit before Thee;
So in mine earthly house I am
　　To that I hope to be.
Break up the Heavens, O Lord! and far
　　Through all yon starlight keen,
Draw me, Thy bride, a glittering star,
　　In raiment white and clean.

He lifts me to the golden doors,
　　The flashes come and go;
All Heaven bursts her starry floors,
　　"And strews her lights below:

And deepens on and up! the gates
   Roll back, and far within
For me the Heavenly bridegroom waits,
   To make me pure of sin.
The Sabbaths of eternity,
   One Sabbath deep and wide,
A light upon the shining sea—
   The bridegroom with his bride!"

The following is from Ulysses:

"I am a part of all that I have met;
Yet all experience is an arch where through
Gleams that untraveled world whose margin fades
Forever and forever when I move.
How dull it is to pause, to make an end,
To rest unburnished not to shine in use!
As though to breathe were life. Life piled on life
Were all too little and of one to me
Little remains; but every hour is saved
From that eternal silence something more,

13

A bringer of new things, and vile it were
For some three suns to store and hoard myself,
And this gray spirit yearning in desire
So follow knowledge like a shining star
Beyond the utmost bound of human thought.

We sometimes find sly veins of humor in Tennyson, a sort of facetiousness that reminds us of Hood. In Will Waterproof's Lyrical monologue we find the following:

"Head-waiter of the chop-house here,
    To which I most resort,
  I too must part: I hold thee dear
    For this good pint of port.
  For this, thou shalt from all things suck
    Marrow of mirth and laughter;
  And, wheresoever thou move, good luck
    Shall fling her old shoe after.

"But thou wilt never move from hence,
  The sphere thy fate allots:
Thy latter days increased with peace,
  Go down among the pots:
Thou battenest by the greasy gleam
  In haunts of hungry sinners,
Old boxes, larded with the steam
  Of thirty thousand dinners.

"*We* fret, *we* fume, would shift our skins,
  Would quarrel with our lot;
Thy care is, under polished tins,
  To serve the hot-and-hot;
To come and go, and come again,
  Returning like the pewit,
And watched by silent gentlemen,
  That trifle with the cruet.

"Live long, e're from thy topmost head
  The thick-set hazel dies;
Long, 'ere the hateful crow shall tread
  The corners of thine eyes;

Nor feel in head or chest
  Our changeful equinoxes,
Till mellow Death, like some late guest,
  Shall call thee from the boxes.

"But when he calls, and thou shall cease
  To pace the gritted floor,
And, laying down an unctuous lease
  Of life, shall earn no more.
No carved cross-bones, the types of Death,
  Shall show thee past to Heaven;
But carved cross-pipes, and, underneath,
  A pint-pot, neatly graven."

In "Maud," he gives us the picture of a
nonchalant gentleman :

"But while I passed he was humming an air,
  Stopt, and then with a riding-whip
Leisurely tapping a glossy boot,
  And curving a contumelious lip,

Gorgonized me from head to foot
With a stony British stare."

He gives us the worth of a vote in the same poem :

"What, if he had told her yester morn,
  How prettily for his own sweet sake,
  A face of tenderness might be feigned,
  And a moist mirage in desert eyes,
  That so, when the rotten hustings shake,
  In another month, to his brazen lies
  A wretched vote may be gained."

In "Aubrey Court" we have a descrip·
tive feast in the pic-nic style :

"There on a slope of orchard, Francis laid
A damask napkin, wrought with horse and hound,
Brought out a dusky loaf that smelt of home,
And, half cut down, a pasty, costly made,

Where quail and pigeon, lark and hornet lay,
Like fossils of the rock, with golden yolks
Imbedded and injellied; last, with these
A flask of cider from his father's vats,
Prime, which I knew; and so we sat and eat,
And talked old matters over."

Among Tennyson's poems, " In Memoriam,'
I find a beautiful epithalamium, supposed
to be inscribed to his daughter, a copious
extract must supply the place of the entire
poem, it being too long for insertion.

"Regret is dead, but love is more
        Than in the summers that are flown,
        For I myself with these have grown
To something greater than before;

" Which makes appear the songs I made
        As echoes out of weaker times,
        As half but idle brawling rhymes,
The sport of random sun and shade.

"But where is she, the bridal flower,
  That must be made a wife 'ere noon ?
  She enters, glowing with the moon
Of Eden on its bridal bower.

"On me she bends her blissful eyes
  And then on thee; they meet thy look,
  And brighten like the star that shook
Betwixt the palms of paradise.

"Oh! when her life was yet in bud,
  He too foretold the perfect rose.
  For thee she grew, for thee she grows,
Forever, and is fair as good.

"And thou art worthy, full of power;
  As gentle, liberal-minded, great,
  Consistent, wearing all that weight
Or leaning lightly like a flower.

"But now set out: the noon is near,
  And I must give away the bride,

She fears not, or with thee beside
And me behind her, will not fear.

"For I that danced her on my knee,
    That watched her on her nurse's arm,
    That shielded all her life from harm,
At last must part with her to thee;

" Now waiting to be made a wife,
    Her feet, my darling, on the dead;
    Their pensive tablets 'round her head,
And the most living words of life

" Breathed in her ear. The ring is on,
    The 'wilt thou' answered, and again
    The 'wilt thou' asked, till out of twain,
Her sweet 'I will' has made ye one.

"Now sign your names, which shall be read,
    Mute symbols of a joyful morn,
    By village eyes as yet unborn;
The names are signed and overhead

" Begins the clash and clang that tells
    The joy to every wandering breeze;
    The blind wall rocks, and on the trees
The dead leaf trembles to the bells.

" O! happy hour! behold the bride
    With him to whom her hand I gave.
    They leave the porch, they pass the grave
That has to-day its sunny side."

THE RELIC OF HAIR.

This golden link of sunny hair
　　Is all that's left of one,
That, like some bright and shining star,
　　Around our pathway shone;
'Twas parted from her fair young brow,
　　Ere death had set his seal
On all the bright and happy flow
　　Which love and hope reveal.

Years in their silent course have fled
　　Since in thy youth and bloom,
With all our love around thee flung,
　　They laid thee in the tomb;
But still thy laugh trills on my ear,
　　Thy form goes floating by

As vividly in memory
  As when it met my eye.

Oh golden tress! that wakes the past,
  Too life-like in my heart,
Where are those sister ringlets now,
  Of which thou formed a part?
Time hath not dimmed its lustrous sheen,
  Though death has robbed the form
Of all the graces which it wore
  In life's bewitching morn?

But though thy tones no more may fall,
  Like music, on my ear,
This golden link shall bid the heart
  Forever hold thee dear.
For, oh! it is a part of thee,
  And well recalls the spell
Whose vivid power on my heart
  Denies a last farewell.

"DEAR MAMMA, I AM NEVER AFRAIL IN THE DARK; ANGELS ARE IN THE DARK."

Yes, when the shadow falleth,
An angels hovers near,
To guard thy little footsteps,
So Maggie need not fear.

And watching o'er her pillow,
And by her cradled bed,
From silent morn till even,
His wings are ever spread.

You do not know his coming,
You do not feel him near,

But 'tis he, my little darling,
  That wipes away the tear.

By whispering words of comfort,
  By urging some redress,
He heals the little sorrow
  That fills my Maggie's breast.

Then love your guardian angel,
  As God's especial friend,
He comes, a special messenger,
  Your footsteps to attend.

TO T. H. D.

My husband, take this little flower,
   And fold him to thy breast,
Look on his baby face and see
   Thy lineaments imprest.

Oh ! smile upon our little child,
   He comes to comfort thee,
To fill a void within thy heart,
   God's blessing on him be.

I ask for this last precious one
   No wreath or titled fame,
But that he bear in noble worth
   Thy dear and honored name,

Oh! for this last best benison,
  Which God to us hath given,
May plenitude of grace be sent,
  To fit his soul for Heaven.

PRETTY BIRDLING.

Little bird, so blithe and gay,
Tilting on the slender spray,
Who so happy, free as you,
Sipping pearls of morning dew?

Tell me, pretty birdie, why
You have left your home so high,
In yon spreading apple tree
And are here so close to me.

So near I watch the expanding throat,
Almost bursting with its note,
Praising Him who rules alway,
For thy short-lived summer day.

Grateful for thy little store,
Never murmuring thou for more,
Yet some wanton, cruel boy
In a moment may destroy,

All thy joys, and scatter wide
The home which love and skill provide,
And thou to fill the bag of game,
Fall victim to the sportsman's aim.

Let man, endowed with reason—sense,
Likened to omnipotence,
Murmuring e'er at God's decree,
Learn the lesson taught by thee!

JOHN KEATS.

All that the imagination can conceive of a poet is to be found in the beautiful portrait of Keats. The high, intellectual forehead, with its clustering curls, those dreamy eyes, the saddened expression which appears to premise a future, ever casting its shadow before, would seem to excite the sympathy as well as admiration of the beholder. Born in obscurity, with surroundings that would vulgarize an ordinary mind, he, by the force of the "divine within him," raised himself above all obstacles to a recognition high, even among the gifted of the land.

Those impediments or barriers which might deter one less earnest were to him incentives. He felt himself to be the arbiter of his own destiny, and he labored with a manly independence and a lofty determination to win for himself the glory of the poet's bay. His life was circled in the short span of twenty-four years. The seeds of disease were sown in his infancy. His days were a struggle between weakness of body and vigor of intellect (averse as this may be to the popular idea of corporeal sympathy, it was in his case nevertheless true), and yet he determined to follow the path of his choice, to win for himself that position from which his lowly lot would seem to debar him.

Keats is best known to us as the author of "Endymion" and "St. Agnes' Eve;" either

one is an immortality.   The opening of
"Endymion" is an earnest of the whole.
As a proof of its beauty, the first line is a
popular quotation :

A thing of beauty is a joy forever:
Its loveliness increases, it will never
Pass into nothingness, but still will keep
A bower quiet for us, and a sleep
Full of sweet dreams and health and quiet breathing."

The pleasure of his muse is told in what
follows :

"Therefore, 'tis with full happiness that I
Will trace the story of Endymion.
The very music of the name has gone
Into my being, and each pleasant scene
Is growing fresh before me as the green
Of our own valleys; so I will begin

Now, while I cannot hear the city's din;
Now while the early budders are just new,
And run in mazes of the youngest hue
About old forests; while the willow trails
In delicate ambers, and the dairy pails
Bring home increase of milk. And as the year
Grows lush in juicy stalks, I'll smoothly steer
My little boat for many quiet hours,
With streams that deepen freshly into bowers.
Many and many a verse I hope to write
Before the daisies, vermeil rimm'd and white,
Hide in deep herbage, and ere yet the bees
Hum about globes of clover and sweet peas,
I must be near the middle of my story.
O, may no wintry season bare and hoary
See it half finished; but let autumn bold,
With universal tinge of sober gold,
Be all about me when I make an end.
And now at once adventuresome I send
My herald thoughts into a wilderness;
There let its trumpet blow and quickly dress

"My uncertain path with green, that I may speed
Easily onward through flowers and weed."

The muse of Keats found a convenient outpouring in the broad field of Grecian mythology. Here he felt free to give utterance to his thoughts. He need not conform to aught but the ideal, and he reveled in the beauties which his own warm fancy and imagination could create. This was his bias. But as a profound thinker on this subject has asserted, "To every poetical mind there seems to be a peculiar nucleus for thought. The sympathies flow in some particular direction; and the glow and imagery of song are excited in a certain manner, according to individual taste and character. To Scott chivalry and all its associations were inspiring; to Wordsworth abstract nature. Cowper loved to group his feelings and fancies round some moral truth; and Pope to weave into verse the phenomena of social life," to Keats we must assign the empire of Grecian mythology. From the world of ideality he gives us the most beautiful sentiments,

There are

Richer entanglements, enthrallments far
More self destroying, leading by degrees
To the chief intensity; the crown of these
Is made of love and friendship, and sits high
Upon the forehead of humanity.
All its more ponderous and bulky worth
Is friendship, whence there ever issues forth
A steady splendor; but at the tip-top
There hangs, by unseen film, an orbed drop
Of light, and that is love; its influence
Thrown in our eyes genders a novel sense,
At which we start and fret, till in the end

Melting, into its radiance we blend,
Mingle and so become a part of it.
Nor with aught else can our souls interknit
So wingedly; when we combine therewith
Life's self is nurtured by its proper pith,
And we are nurtured like a pelican brood.

Endymion in his wandering meets a Naiad,
who guides him on his way, and leaving
him, says :

                    Could I weed
Thy soul of care, by heavens! I would offer
All the bright riches of my crystal coffer
To Amphetrite; all my clear-eyed fish,
Golden or rainbow-sided or purplish,
Vermillion tail'd or finn'd with silvery gauze ·
Yea, or my varied pebbled floor that draws
A virgin light to the deep; my grotto sands,
Tawny and gold oozed slowly from far lands
By my diligent springs; my level lilies, shells,
My charming rod, my potent river spells.

Yes, everything, even to the pearly cup
Meander gave me; for I bubbled up
To fainting creatures in a desert wild.
But wo is me, I am but as a child
To gladden thee, and all I dare to say
Is that I pity thee, that on this day
I've been thy guide; that thou must wander far
In other regions, past the scanty bar
To mortal steps, before thou canst be ta'en
From every wasting sigh, from every pain,
Into the gentle bosom of thy love.
Why it is thus, one knows in Heaven above,
But a poor Naiad, I guess not. Farewell!
I have a ditty for my hollow cell.

Imagination is lavish of her wealth in
this as in all the works of Keats. In his
preface to Endymion, he says, after depre-
cating the attempt to forestall criticism:
" The imagination of a boy is healthy, and

the mature imagination of a man is healthy; but there is a space of life between in which the soul is in a ferment, the character undecided, the way of life uncertain, the ambition thick-sighted; thence proceeds mawkishness and all the thousand bitters which those men I speak of must necessarily taste in going over the following pages. I hope I have not in too late a day touched the beautiful mythology of Greece, and dulled its brightness, for I wish to try once more before I bid it farewell."

The critic of the day, Gifford, declared his intention of attacking Endymion, even before it appeared in print. The effect of this unsparing vituperation upon a morbid state of body may easily be imagined. His being born in a livery stable, and the humble nature of his early antecedents, were crimes too great to be overlooked by lordly rhymers and lofty reverencers. His spirit was gentle, although his soul was strong, and he bore within himself, quietly and uncomplainingly, the obloquies and ridicule which they attempted to cast upon his name. It is true, his education, so far as scholastic teaching was concerned, was confined to a plain, unpretending school at Enfield ; but nature compensated with her gratuitous gifts for want of fortune, and it was conceded by unprejudiced minds that he possessed more exhuberance of fancy, more facility of description, than many of the best English poets of his day.

They must indeed be insensible who feel not the poetic excellence and beauty of some of the following extracts, selected at hazard :

Time, that aged muse,
Rocked me to patience. Now, thank gentle heaven,
The things, with all their comfortings, are given
To my down-sunken hours; and with thee,
Sweet sister, help to stem the ebbing sea
Of weary life.

*   *   *   *   *   *   *   *   *

O! magic sleep! O! comfortable bird,
That broodest o'er the troubled sea of the mind
Till it is hushed and smooth! O! unconfined,
Restraint, imprisoned liberty, great key
To golden palaces, strange minstrelsy,
Fountains grotesque, new trees, bespangled caves,
Echoing grottoes, fall of tumbling waves,
And moonlight; ay, to all the mazy world
Of silvery enchantment; who unfurled
Beneath thy drowsy wing a triple hour,
But renovates and lives.

*   *   *   *   *   *   *   *   *

ɔudden a thought came like a full-blown rose,
Flushed his brow, and in his pained heart
Made purple riot.

Now, indeed,
His senses had swooned off; he did not heed
The sudden silence or the whispers low,
Or the old eyes dissolving at his woe,
Or anxious calls, or close of trembling palms,
Or maiden's sigh, that grief itself embalms.

* * * * * * * * *

Do not all charms fly
At the mere touch of cold philosophy?
There was an awful rainbow once in heaven;
We know her woof, her texture; she is given
In the dull catalogue of common things.
Philosophy will clip an angel's wings,
Conquer all mysteries by rule and line,
Empty the haunted air, the gnomed mine.

* * * * * * * * *

Of wealthy lustre was the banquet room,
Filled with pervading brilliance and perfnme;
Before each lucid panel fuming stood
A censor, fed with myrrh and spiced wood,
Each by a sacred tripod held aloft,
Whose slender feet wide swerved upon the soft
Wool woofed carpets. Fifty wreaths of smoke
From fifty censors their light voyage took,
To the high roof, still mimicked as they rose
Along the mirror'd walls, by twin clouds odorous.
Twelve sphered tables, by silk seats ensphered,
High as the level of a man's breast, reared
On libbard's paws, upheld the heavy gold
Of cups and goblets, and the store thrice told
Of Ceres horn, and in huge vessels wine
Came from the gloomy tun with merry shine.

*　*　*　*　*　*　*　*　*

What is there in thee, Moon, that thou shouldst move
My heart so potently? When yet a child
I oft have dried my tears when thou hast smiled.

Thou seem'dst my sister: hand in hand we went
From eve to morn across the firmament.
No apples would I gather from the tree

Till thou had'st cooled their cheeks deliciously:
No tumbling water ever spake romance
But when my eyes with thine thereon could dance;

No woods were green enough, no bower divine
Until thou lifted'st up thine eyeslids fine;
In sowing time ne'er would I dibble take,
Or drop a seed till thou wast wide awake;
And in the summer-tide of blossoming
No one but thee hath heard me blithely sing,
And mesh my dewy flowers all the night;
No melody was like a passing sprite
If I went not to solemnize thy reign.
Yes, in my boyhood, every joy and pain
By thee were fashion'd to the self-same aim;
As I grew in years, still did'st thou blend
With all my ardors: thou wast the deep glen;

Thou wast the mountain-top—the sage's pen—
The poet's harp—the voice of friends—the sun,
Thou wast the river—thou wast glory won;
Thou wast my clarion's blast—thou wast my steed—
My goblet full of wine—my topmost deed;
Thou wast the charm of woman, lovely Moon,
O, what a wild and harmonized tune
My spirit struck from all the beautiful!
On some bright essence could I lean and lull
Myself to immortality.

Milne tells us that while at Enfield, Keats' translations, during the last two years of his stay, were astonishing. The twelve books of the Eneid were a portion of it. To Tooke's Pantheon, Spence's Polymetis and Sempriese's Dictionary, we are indebted, for his deep and extended knowledge of mythology. Of the Hyperion, a poem full of the "large utterance of the early gods," Shelley

has said, that the scenery and drawing of
Saturn dethroned by the fallen Titans, sur-
passed those of Satan and his rebellious
angels in Paradise Lost. Keats thought
lightly of many of his own finest productions. His "Ode to a Nightingale," which
was first published in the "Annals of Fine
Arts," he thrust aside as waste paper, and
some difficulty occurred in arranging, from
the often mutilated fragments, the stanzas
in anything like order. He frequently would
chant, in a sort of recitative, those that
most suited his fancy, and the impression of
his enthusiasm and manner were afterwards
never forgotten by those who were privi-
leged to listen to him. Of his "St. Agnes'
Eve," he thus writes to his brother : "I took
down some thin paper, and wrote on it—
wrote a little poem called St. Agnes' Eve

—which you will have as it is, when I have finished the blank part of the rest for you."

Jeffrey thus criticises this gem of English literature : — "The glory and charm of the poem is the description of the fair maiden's antique chamber, and of all that passes in that sweet and angel guarded sanctuary, every part of which is touched with colors at once high and delicate, and the whole chastened and harmonized in the midst of its gorgeous distinctness, by a pervading grace and purity that indicate not less clearly the exaltation than the refinement of the author's fancy." The poem, though long, is given entire :

THE EVE OF ST. AGNES.

St. Agnes' Eve—ah, bitter chill it was!
The owl, for all his feathers was a-cold;
The hare limp'd trembling through the frozen grass,
And silent was the flock in woolly fold;
Numb were the beadsman's fingers while he told
His rosary, and while his frosted breath,
Like pious incense from a censer old,
Seemed taking flight for Heaven without a death,
Past the sweet Virgin's picture, while his prayer he saith.

His prayer he saith, this patient, holy man;
Then takes his lamp, and riseth from his knees,
And back returneth, meagre, barefoot, wan,
Along the chapel aisle by slow degrees;
The sculptured dead, on each side seem to freeze,
Emprison'd in black, purgatorial rails;
Knights, ladies, praying in dumb orat'ries,
He passeth by; and his weak spirit fails
To think how they may ache in icy hoods and mails.

Northward he turneth through a little door,
And scarce three steps, ere music's golden tongue
Flatter'd to tears this aged man and poor;
But no, already had his death-bell rung;
The joys of all his life were said and sung:
His was harsh penance on St. Agnes' Eve;
Another way he went, and soon among
Rough ashes sat he for his soul's reprieve,
And all night kept awake, for sinners' sake to grieve.

That ancient Beadsman heard the prelude soft ·
And so it chanced for many a door was wide,
From hurry to and fro. Soon, up aloft,
The silver, snarling trumpets 'gan to chide ,
The level chambers, ready with their pride,
Were glowing to receive a thousand guests;
The carved angels, ever eager-eyed,
Stared, where upon their heads the cornice rests,
With hair blown back, and wings put cross-wise on their
    breast.

At length burst in the argent revelry,
With plumes, tiara, and all rich array,

Numerous as shadows haunting fairily

The brain, new stuff'd, in youth, with triumphs gay

Of old romance. These let us wish away,

And turn, sole-thoughted, to one Lady there,

Whose heart had brooded, all that wintry day,

On love, and wing'd St. Agnes' saintly care,

As she had heard old dames full many times declare.

They told her how, upon St. Agnes' Eve,

Young virgins might have visions of delight,

And soft adornings from their loves receive

Upon the honey'd middle of the night,

If ceremonies due they did aright;

As supperless to bed they must retire,

And couch supine their beauties, lily white;

Nor look behind, nor sideways, but require

Of Heaven, with upward eyes, for all that they desire.

Full of this whim was thoughtful Madeline;

The music, yearning like a God in pain,

She scarcely heard; her maiden eyes divine,

Fixed on the floor, saw many a sweeping train

Pass by—she heeded not at all; in vain
Came many a tip-toe, amorous cavalier,
And back retired; not cooled by high disdain,
But she saw not; her heart was otherwhere;
She sigh'd for Agnes' dreams, the sweetest of the year.

She danced along with vague, regardless eyes,
Anxious her lips, her breathing quick and short,
The hallow'd hour was near at hand; she sighs
Amid the timbrels, and the throng'd resort
Of whisperers in anger, or in sport;
'Mid looks of love, defiance, hate, and scorn,
Hoodwink'd with fairy fancy; all amost,
Save to St. Agnes and her lambs unshorn,
And all the bliss to be before the morrow morn.

So, purposing each moment to retire,
She linger'd still. Meantime across the moors,
Had come young Porphyro, with heart on fire
For Madeline. Beside the portal doors,
Buttress'd from moonlight, stands he, and implores
All saints to give him sight of Madeline,

But for one moment in the tedious hours,

That he might gaze and worship all unseen;

Perchance, speak, kneel, touch, kiss—in sooth such things
    have been.

He ventures in : let no buzz'd whispers tell·

All eyes be muffled or a hundred swords

Will storm his heart, love's feverous citadel

For him, those chambers held barbarian hordes,

Hyena foemen, and hot-blooded lords,

Whose very dogs would execrations howl,

Against his lineage ; not one breast affords

Him any mercy, in that mansion foul,

Save one old beldame, weak in body and in soul.

Ah, happy chance ! the aged creature came,

Shuffling along with ivory-headed wand,

To where he stood, hid from the torch's flame,

Behind a broad hall-pillar, far beyond

The sound of merriment and chorus bland;

He startled her; but soon she knew his face,

And grasp'd his fingers in her palsied hand,

Saying, " Mercy, Prophyro! hie thee from this place,
They are all here to-night, the whole blood-thirsty race!

" Get hence! get hence! there's dwarfish Hildebrand;
He had a fever late, and in the fit,
He cursed thee and thine, both house and land;
Then there's that old lord Maurice, not a whit
More tame for his grey hairs—alas me! flit!
Flit like a ghost away."—"Ah, Gossip dear,
We're safe enough! here in this arm-chair sit,
And tell me how."—" Good saints! not here, not here,
Follow me, child, or else these stones will be thy bier."

He followed through a lowly arched way,
Brushing the cobwebs with his lofty plume;
And as she mutter'd " Well, a-well-a-day,"
He found him in a little moonlight room,
Pale, latticed, chill, and silent as a tomb.
"Now tell me where is Madeline," said he,
" Oh tell me, Angela, by the holy loom
Which none but sacred sisterhood may see,
When they St. Agnes' wool are weaving piously."

"St. Agnes! ah! it is St. Agnes' Eve—
Yet men will murder upon holy days;
Thou must hold water in a witch's sieve,
And be liege-lord of all the Elves and Fays.
To venture so ; it fills me with amaze
To see thee, Porphyro! St. Agnes' Eve!
God's help! my lady fair, the conjuror plays,
This very night good angels her deceive !
But let me laugh awhile, I've mickle time to grieve."

Feebly she laughed in the languid moon,
While Porphyro upon her face doth look,
Like puzzled urchin on an aged crone
Who keepeth closed a wondrous riddle-book,
As spectacled she sits in chimney nook.
But soon his eyes grew brilliant, when she told
His lady's purpose; and he scarce could brook
Tears, at the thought of those enchantments cold,
And Madeline asleep in lap of legends old.

Sudden a thought came like a full-blown rose,
Flushing his brow, and his pained heart

Made purple riot; then doth he propose
A stratagem, that makes the beldame start:
"A cruel man and impious thou art;
Sweet lady, let her pray, and sleep and dream,
Alone with her good angels, far apart
From wicked men like thee. Go, go! I deem
Thou canst not surely be same that thou didst seem."

"I will not harm her, by all saints I swear,"
Quoth Porphyro; "O may I ne'er find grace
When my weak voice shall whisper its last prayer,
If one of her soft ringlets I displace,
Or look with ruffian passion in her face.
Good Angela, believe me by these tears;
Or I will, even in a moment's space,
Awake with horrid shout my foeman's ears,
And beard them, though they be more fang'd than
    wolves and bears."

"Ah! why wilt thou affright a feeble soul?
A poor, weak, palsy-stricken, churchyard thing,
Whose passing-bell may ere the midnight toll;

Whose prayers for thee, each morn and evening,
Were never miss'd." Thus plaining does she bring
A gentler speech from burning Porphyro ;
So woful, and of such deep sorrowing,
That Angela gives promise that she will do
Whatever he shall wish, betide her weal or wo.

Which was, to lead him, in close secrecy,
Even to Madeline's chamber, and there hide
Him in a closet, of such privacy
That he might see her beauty unespied,
And win, perhaps, that night a peerless bride,
While legion'd fairies paced the coverlet,
And pale enchantment held her sleepy-eyed.
Never on such a night have lovers met,
Since Merlin paid his Demon all the monstrous debt.

"It shall be as thou wishest," said the Dame;
"All cates and dainties shall be stored there
Quickly on the feast-night: by the tambour frame
Her own lute thou wilt see: no time to spare,
For I am slow and feeble, and scarce dare

On such a catering trust my dizzy head.
Wait here, my child, with patience, kneel in prayer
The while: Ah! thou must needs the lady wed,
Or may I never leave my grave among the dead."

So saying, she hobbled off with busy fear,
The lover's endless minutes slowly pass'd;
The dame return'd, and whisper'd in his ear
To follow her; with aged eyes aghast
From fright of dim especial. Safe at last,
Through many a dusky gallery, they gain
The maiden's chamber, silken, hush'd and chaste;
Where Porphyro took covert, pleased amain.
His poor guide hurried back with agues in her brain

Her faltering hand upon the balustrade.
Old Angela was feeling for the stair,
When Madeline, St. Agnes' charmed maid,
Rose, like a mission'd spirit, unaware:
With silver taper's light, and pious care,
She turn'd, and down the aged gossip led
To a safe level matting. Now prepare,

Young Porphyro, for gazing on that bed ;
She comes, she comes again, like ring-dove fray'd and
    fled.

Out went the taper, as she hurried in ;
Its little smoke, in pallid moonshine, died ;
She closed the door, she panted, all akin
To spirits of the air, and visions wide ;
No utter'd syllable, or, wo betide !
But to her heart, her heart was voluble,
Paining with eloquence her balmy side ;
As though a tongueless nightingale should swell
Her throat in vain, and die, heart-stifled, in her dell.

A casement high and triple-arched there was,
All garlanded with carven imageries
Of fruits and flowers, and bunches of knot-grass,
And diamonded with panes of quaint device,
Innumerable of stains and splendid dyes,
As are the tiger-moth's deep damask'd wings ;
And in the midst, 'mong thousand heraldries,
And twilight saints, and dim emblazonings,
A childlike scutcheon blush'd with blood of kings and
    queens.

Full on this casement shone the wintry moon,
And threw warm gules on Madeline's fair breast,
As down she knelt for heaven's grace and boon ;
Rose-bloom fell on her hands, together prest,
And on her silver cross soft amethyst,
And on her hair a glory, like a saint :
She seem'd a splendid angel, newly drest,
Save wings, for heaven.   Porphyro grew faint :
She knelt, so pure a thing, so free from mortal taint.

Anon his heart revives ; her vespers done,
Of all its wreathed pearls her hair she frees ;
Unclasps her warmed jewels one by one ;
Loosens her fragrant bodice ; by degrees
Her rich attire creeps rustling to her knees :
Half-hidden, like a mermaid in sea-weed,
Pensive awhile she dreams awake, and sees,
In fancy, fair St. Agnes in her bed,
But dares not look behind, or all the charm is fled.

Soon, trembling in her soft and chilly nest,
In sort of wakeful swoon, perplex'd she lay,

Until the poppied warmth of sleep oppress'd
Her soothed limbs, and soul fatigued away;
Flown, like a thought until the morrow-day;
Blissfully haven'd both from joy and pain;
Clasp'd like a missal where swart Paynims pray;
Blinded alike from sunshine and from rain,
As though a rose should shut, and be a bud again.

Stolen to this paradise, and so entranced,
Porphyro gazed upon her empty dress,
And listen'd to her breathing, if it chanced
To wake into a slumberous tenderness;
Which, when he heard, that minute did he bless,
And breathed himself; then from the closet crept,
Noiseless as fear in a wilderness,
And over the hush'd carpet, silent, stept,
And 'tween the curtains peep'd, where, lo! how fast
    she slept.

Then by the bed-side, where the faded moon
Made a dim, silver twilight, soft he set

A table, and, half anguish'd, threw thereon
A cloth of woven crimson gold, and jet :—
O for some drowsy Morphean amulet !
The boisterous, midnight, festive clarion,
The kettle-drum, and far-heard clarionet,
Affray his ears, though but in dying tone :—
The hall-door shuts again, and all the noise is gone.

And still she slept an azure-lidded sleep,
In blanched linen, smooth, and lavender'd,
While he from forth the closet brought a heap
Of candied apple, quince, and plum, and gourd ;
With jellies smoother than the creamy curd,
And lucent syrups, tinct with cinnamon ;
Manna and dates, in argosy transferr'd
From Fez ; and spiced dainties, every one,
From silken Samarcand to cedar'd Lebanon.

These delicates he heap'd with glowing hand
On golden dishes and in baskets bright
Of wreathed silver : sumptuous they stand
In the retired quiet of the night,

Filling the chilly room with perfume light.
"And now, my love, my seraph fair, awake!
Thou art my heaven, and I thine eremite:
Open thine eyes, for meek St. Agnes' sake,
Or I shall drowse beside thee, so my soul doth ache."

Thus whispering, his warm, unnerved arm
Sank in her pillow. Shaded was her dream
By the dusk curtains:—'t was a midnight charm
Impossible to melt as iced stream:
The lustrous salvers in the moonlight gleam;
Broad golden fringe upon the carpet lies;
It seem'd he never, never could redeem
From such a steadfast spell his lady's eyes;
So mused awhile, entoiled in woofed phantasies.

Awakening up, he took her hollow lute,—
Tumultuous,—and, in chords that tenderest be,
He play'd an ancient ditty, long since mute,
In Provence call'd "La belle dame sans merci,"
Close to her ear touching the melody;
Wherewith disturb'd, she utter'd a soft moan;

16

He ceased—she panted quick—and suddenly
Her blue affrayed eyes wide open shone;
Upon his knees he sank, pale as smooth-sculptured
    stone.

Her eyes were open, but she still beheld,

Now wide awake, the vision of her sleep.

There was a painful change, that nigh expell'd

The blisses of her dream so pure and deep,

At which fair Madeline began to weep,

And moan forth witless words with many a sigh;

While still her gaze on Porphyro would keep;

Who knelt, with joined hands and piteous eye,

Fearing to move or speak, she look'd so dreamingly.

"Ah, Porphyro!" said she, "but even now

Thy voice was at sweet tremble in mine ear,

Made tuneable with every sweetest vow,

And those sad eyes were spiritual and clear;

How changed thou art! how pallid, chill, and drear!

Give me that voice again, my Porphyro,

Those looks immortal, those complainings dear!

Oh, leave me not in this eternal woe,
For if thou diest, my love, I know. not where to go."

Beyond a mortal man, impassion'd far
At these volumptuous accents, he arose,
Ethereal, flush'd, and like a throbbing star
Seen 'mid the sapphire heaven's deep repose;
Into her dream he melted, as the rose
Blendeth its odor with the violet,—
Solution sweet; meantime the frost-wind blows
Like Love's alarm pattering the sharp sleet
Against the window-panes; St. Agnes' noon hath set.

'Tis dark; quick pattereth the flaw-blown sleet;
"This is no dream, my bride, my Madeline!"
'Tis dark; the iced gusts still rave and beat.
"No dream, alas! alas! and woe is mine!
Porphyro will leave me here to fade and pine.
Cruel! what traitor could thee hither bring?
I curse not, for my heart is lost in thine,
Though thou forsakest a deceived thing—
A dove forlorn and lost with sick unpruned wing."

"My Madeline! sweet dreamer! lovely bride!
Say, may I be for aye thy vassal blest?
Thy beauty's shield, heart-shaped and vermeil dyed?
Ah, silver shrine, here will I take my rest
After so many hours of toil and quest,
A famished pilgrim—saved by miracle.
Though I have found, I will not rob thy nest
Saving of thy sweet self, if thou think'st well
To trust, fair Madeline, to no rude infidel."

"Hark! 'tis an elfin-storm from fairy land,
Of haggard seeming, but a boon indeed;
Arise! arise! the morning is at hand;
The bloated wassailers will never heed.
Let us away, my love, with happy speed;
There are no ears to hear, or eyes to see.
Drown'd all in Rhenish and the sleepy mead;
Awake! arise! my love, and fearless be,
For o'er the southern moors I have a home for thee."

She hurried at his words, beset with fears,
For there were sleeping dragons all around,

At glaring watch, perhaps with ready spears—
Down the wide stairs a darkling way they found,
In all the house was heard no human sound.
A chain-droop'd lamp was flickering by each door;
The arras, rich with horseman, hawk and hound,
Flutter'd in the besieging wind's uproar;
And the long carpets rose along the gusty floor.

They glide, like phantoms, into the wide hall;
Like phantoms to the iron porch they glide,
Where lay the porter,-in uneasy sprawl,
With a huge empty flagon by his side;
The wakeful blood-hound rose, and shook his hide,
But his sagacious eye an inmate owns;
By one, and one, the bolts full easy slide;
The chains lie silent on the foot-worn stones;
The key turns, and the door upon its hinges groans.

And they are gone; ay, ages long ago,
These lovers fled away into the storm.
That night the Baron dreamt of many a wo,
And all his warrior-guests, with shade and form

Of witch, and demon, and large coffin-worm,
Were long be-nightmared. Angela, the old,
Died palsy-twitch'd, with meagre face deform ;
The Beadsman, after thousand aves told,
For aye unsought-for slept among his ashes cold.

A biographer says : " It was the intention of Keats to diffuse the coloring of 'St. Agnes' Eve ' throughout a poem in which character and sentiment would be the figures to such drapery." He did not live to carry out this plan. The quantity of his writings is very remarkable, when we consider how short a life was vouchsafed him.

Often melancholy from his failing health, he was not to be persuaded from the thought of an early death. He possessed in a remarkable degree that self-prescience of disease which stopped for days together the rich stream of fancy and the glowing imagery of thought. He said once to his friend, Mr. Brown: "Flatter me with a hope of happiness when I shall be well, for I am now so weak that I can be flattered into hope."

In a letter to Mr. Bailey, he says: "I have written fifteen hundred lines in two months, most of which, besides many more of prior composition, you will probably see by next winter. One of my ambitions is to make as great a revolution in modern dramatic writing as Kean has done in acting. I am convinced every day that (excepting the human-friend philosopher,) a fine writer is the most genuine being in the world. Shakspeare and the 'Paradise Lost' every day become greater wonders to me. I look upon fine phrases like a lover."

When we consider what this noble and
gifted son of poetry might have been had
he possessed the bodily strength so necessary for any excellence or preferment, we
feel still more the almost fiendish injustice
of his persecutors, who, with insatiable mo-
tive, would deprive him of his peace of
mind and discourage all attempts at future
excellence. Before considering their at-
tacks, it is almost a comfort to know the
character of his enemies, the following from
a reliable source : " The reviewers of Blackwood and the Quarterly were persons evi-
dently destitute of all poetic perception, di-
recting an unrefined and unscrupulous satire
against political opponents, whose intellectual merits they had no means of understanding. The Quarterly admits that he had
not read, or could not read the work he .

undertook to criticise. This impertinence should have prevented the article from having any weight. The Blackwood sought to be facetious, and tells Keats, "It is a better and wiser thing to be a starved apothecary, (alluding to the time he spent with a surgeon,) than a starved poet," and he bids him "back to his gallipot." How bright and beautiful by contrast shine forth the remarks of Jeffreys, who, after pointing out the great excellences of Endy-mion, finishes by saying we do not know any book which we would sooner employ as a test to ascertain whether any one had in him a native relish for poetry and a genuine sensibility to its intrinsic charm. Byron regarded this praise with jealous discontent at first, but afterwards says, "This (Keats') fragment of Hyperion seems

actually inspired by the Titians, and is sublime as Eschylus." Shelley, who loved
Keats as a brother, was indignant with the
Quarterly, and says the Endymion should
not have been noticed at all, except for the
purpose of bringing its excellences into
notice, and continues: "I speak impartially,
for the canons of taste to which Keats has
conformed in his other compositions, are the
very reverse of my own." He describes the
agony of the poet upon reading the article
in question, and adds: "It has induced a
disease from the recovery of which there is
but little hope." Many of the friends of
Keats denied such effects upon his mind
and system, and in justification quote letters from him written at this time.

He says in one of these: "I have read
the papers, and feel indebted to those gen-

tlemen who have taken my part. I will
write independently. I have done so per
haps without judgment. Hereafter I will
write independently, with judgment. I was
never afraid of failure, for I would sooner
fail than not to be among the greatest."
This certainly does not sound like one who
takes the subject much to heart; but his
brother tells us: "After all, Blackwood and
the Quarterly, associated with our family
disease, consumption, were ministers of death
sufficiently venomous, cruel and deadly to
have consigned one of less sensibility to a
premature grave."

In the hope of prolonging a life which
was consuming itself by its own ardent
longings, Keats embarked for Italy. A dear
and tender friend accompanied him. Soothed
and cheered by his gentle ministrations, his

life ebbed slowly away. When vitality seemed exhausted, his spirit appeared to rally again and again the dying energy of his nature, and re-animate itself in death. Gentleness and submission, patience and resignation, were his crowning virtues, and as the death damps were gathering on his brow he whispered to his friend his epitaph: "My name was writ in water." A plain white stone marks the last resting place of this young and gifted son of poetry. Thither has many a pilgrimage been taken. The last recognition has been freely given when he could no longer be soothed by caresses or stimulated by approval, and now—

"He has outsoared the shadow of our night,
Envy and calumny, and hate and pain,

And that unrest which men miscall delight,

Can touch him not and torture not again.

From the contagion of the world's slow stain

He is secure, and now can never mourn

A heart grown cold, a head grown gray in vain.

Nor when the spirit's self has ceased to burn,

With sparkless ashes load an unlamented urn."

LA SOEUR DE CHARITÉ.

—

Whence art thou, being of seraphic mould,
    With thy calm brow and deep religious eye,
And arms thus folded on thy breast,
    Thy mission truly cometh from the sky

What love divine, what charity sublime,
    Didst nerve thy purpose and inflame thy will,
The high resolves borne in that sainted face,
    An added zeal in every breast instil?

Did'st thou not leave in some bright happy home,
    A father's blessing and a mother's voice,
A sister's twining arms, a brother's love,
    Whose coming made thy heart rejoice?

Do not dear memories of that happy band,
  Darken the sunshine of thy placid brow,
Those gentle visitants of by-gone hours,
  With their soft pleadings, musical and low?

I know thou'rt human, for I've seen thee weep,
  When bending o'er the sufferer's couch of pain,
Until thy pity waked some gentle chord,
  Soft tuned with confidence and trust again.

I know thou'rt loving, for I've seen thee fold
  The helpless orphan in thy shielding arm,
Hush her low sobbings into peaceful rest,
  · And shield her innocence from guilt or harm.

But some there are who knew thee when
  Genius and fortune bent the knee,
And worshipped at thy beauty's shrine,
  With love, almost idolatry.

In scenes of pleasure, pomp and pride,
  Thy gentle spirit could not rest,
For thoughts of Jesus crucified,
  Were ever burning in thy breast.

And when the tones of mirth flashed high,
  And music thrilled its sweetest lay,
A whisper low had pierced thy heart,
  Which called thee hence, away! away!

Responsive to that holy call,
  All lesser love is now forgot,
The world may deem it strange and wild,
  Her prayers are heard, she recks it not.

The costly gem is laid aside,
  The curls are severed from her brow,
Madonna-like, a simple veil,
  Half hides its classic beauty now.

Let's follow her to scenes of woe,
   The hireling nurse has fled with fear,
But still her place is not bereft,
   A gentler form is hovering near.

Oh! listen, listen to her prayer,
   Can Heaven withstand that sweet appeal?
Oh! no, for down those faded cheeks,
   The thickly coursing tear-drops steal!

And here we leave her 'mid those scenes,
   And dangers which might well appal,
With angels for her guardian shield,
   The dauntless child of Vincent Paul.

IN MEMORIAM.

Clasped within our heart of hearts,
As the petals of the rose
Fold the golden pollen close,
Tender in its warm repose.

So our Grace,* our household treasure,
Fonder loved from day to day,
Till our Father saw the measure,
Stole from Him our hearts away.

Then when day was closing o'er us,
In the shadowy evenfall,
When the heart with love is tender,
When she dearest seemed to all—

---

* "Our Grace" died April 9, 1861.

Came a youth with noiseless footsteps;
  Ambient shone his floating hair,
And upon her pale, pale forehead
  Laid the crown which seraphs wear.

"Earth's no longer ours forever!"
  Sang he this exulting strain,
And our darling's tiny numbers
  Mingled with the sweet refrain.

Now each heart is bowed in anguish,
  But amid the sorrow dim
Feel they that our Lord hath spoken,
  And they yield her back to Him.

NURSERY SONG.

Sleep, gently sleep, my baby boy,
  For happy dreams are thine;
I know it by the token old.
  Then sleep, sweet baby mine.

Thy head is pillowed on my breast,
  In passive slumbering it lies:
The shadow of an angel's wing
  Enfolds thy dreamy eyes.

'Tis sweet to press thee closely thus,
  And note the beating time
With which thy little throbbing heart
  Responds each pulse of mine.

Then gently sleep, my baby boy,
  In happy visions blest.
While softly rests thy golden head
  Upon a mother's breast.

TO S. M. R.

My sister friend, 'tis joy to think
That in thy far off city home
These simple lines may wake a thought,
A memory of your absent one.

And when you read, perchance will say—
Ah me! I wish that, as in days of yore,
I could by glancing o'er the street,
Just see her standing at the door.

How often, just as day-light closed,
We met for converse grave and gay,
My children playing at your feet,
We passed a happy hour away.

I always met a welcome kind,
  I always felt your clasped hand,
Your love and time hath proved it well,
  Was ever free at my command.

We reveled with the poets old,
  Roamed in their dreamland far away,
Then laughed and said, the brow may sere
  And yet the heart be young alway.

Another one, I mind me well,
  With soul from all but us apart,
Is fanning now through time and space,
  The smouldering embers of my heart.

Our past hath had its sombre clouds,
  But oftentimes the glorious blue,
With silver lining, would shine out,
  And burst the murky darkness through.

Then in this view let's be content,
　Nor willingly admit the ill,
That better in the plan of life
　We may our Maker's hest fulfil.

ROBERT BURNS.

Robert Burns was born on the 29th of September, 1759, in a cottage (or what was more frequently called a "clay bigging") about two miles from the city of Ayr, in Scotland. He was a peasant and the son of a peasant. As early as his sixth year he betrayed a fondness for books; although his supply was scanty, he seemed ever engaged in his favorite occupation of reading, and it is probable he read and digested again and again until he made the limited matter his own. At the age of thirteen he was sent to a rather advanced school, where he acquired some French and a little Latin, but the pecuniary difficulties of his father, who in attempting to better his condition had involved himself in speculations ruinous to his family, obliged our poet to leave school at an early age and employ himself in the occupation of husbandry. He seems to have felt acutely the troubles of the family, and the depression of spirits which affected him at this time appears to have impressed his future career, for he was ever after subject to moods of depression. He had the misfortune to lose his good father at an early age, and the future maintenance of the family became almost exclusively his sole charge. His beautiful tribute of affection for that revered parent, for whom he always entertained the most honorable respect and filial piety, conveys the grateful testimony of a devoted child :

O ye whose cheek the tear of pity stains,
    Draw near with pious reverence and attend.
Here lie the loving husband's dear remains,
    The tender father and the generous friend,
The pitying heart that felt for human woe,
    The dauntless heart that feared no human pride,
The friend of man, to vice alone a foe,
    "For e'en his failings leaned to virtue's side."

As he expresses it : " I first committed the sin of rhyming at the age of fifteen." A young female who assisted him in the labors of the field having inspired a boyish affection, he composed a song descriptive of her charms. Even in this, his first attempt, the poet seems older than the boy, for he was then but an ungainly, awkward boy, entirely unacquainted with men and the manners of the world, but yet so bent on the prosecution of his fancy, combined with a desire for improvement, that from his seventeenth to his twenty-first year he made considerable literary attainment. Burns was distinguished by a strong and vigorous mind, a spirit untamable, a resentment quick, and a perception of right which, if ever invaded, roused him to the most scathing and violent vituperation. He possessed a perfect scorn for deceit or dissimulation, and his muse was ever the friend of the oppressed. How beautifully he asks the charitable sympathy of the world on the unfortunate:

> Then gently scan your brother man,
> Still gentler sister woman;

Tho' they may gang a kennin wrang,
  To step aside is human;
One point must still be greatly dark,
  The moving *why* they do it;
And just as lamely can ye mark
  How far perhaps they rue it.

Who made the heart, 'tis He alone
  Decidedly can try us;
He knows each chord—its various tone,
  Each spring, its various bias;
Then at the balance let's be mute,
  We never can adjust it;
What's done we partly may compute,
  But know not what's resisted.

No more touching advocacy could be
found than the above, joined as it is with
a simplicity so refreshing and beautiful.
To the preservation of this his rustic life

was eminently favorable, and as generosity and benevolence form the sentiment of Burns' muse, so entire truthfulness constitutes the charm which demands our approbation. A child could not speak more frankly of his feelings than the following:

Just now I've ta'en the fit o' rhyme,
My Barnie noddle's working prime,
My fancy yerkit up sublime
    Wi' hasty summon;
Hae ye a leisure moment's time
    To hear what's comin'?

Yet with all his simplicity, nay, even rusticity, he maintained his position with dignity, even among the polished circles of Edinburgh.

Unfortunately, it must be acknowledged he sometimes permitted his social habits to

overstep the bounds of prudence, and allowed himself to be seduced, by pressing
invitations, into the society of those whose
conviviality, without being gross, was too
free to be considerate. The indulgencies
of his festive companions were exhilara-
tions of pleasure at his success, and a generous mind has often found it difficult to
resist a temptation under such circumstances. His appearance at this time is
described as remarkably interesting. His
form was finely developed, and indicated
masculine vigor and agility; his ample
forehead was shaded with a profusion of
curls ; his eyes were large, dark and full;
his face was well-formed, and his whole
countenance extremely pleasing ; his conversation was fascinating ; his sallies of wit
and humor irresistible. But these qualities

left him often a prey to a certain class of persons, who sought his genius as a sanction to their excessive indulgences. Yet no man ever felt his own imperfections more than Burns. He knew and lamented them; while the spirit of independence which he maintained prevented him from ever being the tool of the politician, or the toady of the great. He had a desire to raise his family from their condition, which, though it was elevated by the genius of the father, often felt the inconveniences of a limited income. To one who befriended him in this laudable desire, he has addressed himself in terms of undying gratitude. The concluding verses of his poem, "The Lament for James, Earl of Glencairn," (his benefactor), are particularly fine:

In poverty's low barren vale,
  Thick mists obscure involve me round,
Though oft I turned the wistful eye,
  Nae ray of fame was to be found.
Thou foundst me, like the morning sun
  That melts the fogs in limped air,
The friendless bard and rustic song,
  Became alike thy fostering care.   .

O why has worth so short a date,
  While vilians ripen gray with time;
Must thou, the noble, generous, great,
  Fall in bold manhood's hardy prime.
Why did I live to see that day,
  A day to me so full of woe;
O, had I met the mortal shaft
  Which laid my benefactor low.

The bridegroom may forget the bride,
  Was made his wedded wife yestreen;

> The monarch may forget the crown
>> That on his head an hour hath been;
> The mother may forget the child
>> That smiles sae sweetly on her knee;
> But I'll remember thee, Glencairn,
>> And a' that thou hast done for me.

Truly has Robert Burns been called "the heir of fame, but the child of sorrow." After the public and universal recognition of his genius, it might be expected that an attempt would at least be made to place him in circumstances favorable to its further development; but in this he was most wofully disappointed. His expectations were not very extravagant. He only asked a situation where his exertions might be uninterrupted by the fatigues of labor and the calls of want; and he said "a life of literary leisure, with a decent competence, is the summit of my wishes." "The happiest, indeed, are they of whom Fame speaks not with her clarion voice." The humble labors of a farm, the monotonous serenity of an agricultural life, became weary to the erratic fancies and the poetic temperament of Burns. Then his utter ignorance of management, his want of tact and skill in the little requisites necessary to success, were a constant source of trouble and embarassment to him. Under the pressure of such circumstances he sought and obtained the humble position of gauger or exciseman of the district in which he lived. Dr. Currie, his biographer, describes his farm as in a great measure abandoned to his servants, while he betook himself to the duties of his new appointment. He might

still, indeed, be seen in the spring, direct-
ing his plow, a labor in which he excelled;
or with a white sheet containing his seed
corn slung across his shoulders, striding
with measured steps along his turned up
furrows, and scattering the grain in the
earth. But the farm no longer occupied
the principal part of his care or of his
thoughts. It was not at Ellisland that he
was now in general to be found. Mounted
on horseback, this high-minded poet was
pursuing the defaulters of the revenue
among the hills and vales of Nithsdale, his
roving eye wandering over the charms of
nature, and muttering his wayward fancies
as he moved along. But oh, how sadly
does his new career at Dumfries contrast
with the inspired peasant and faithful limner of an humble lot. His temptations

were too strong for his weak purposes, and his resolutions were constantly overcome by the "killing kindness of his friends." In moments of quiet and thought he however produced some admirable compositions, and still went on advancing his poetic fame. His own description of a poet's fate is no inapt illustration of his own:

Creatures though oft the prey of care and sorrow,
When blest to-day unmindful of to morrow;
A being formed t' amuse his graver friends,
Admired and praised—and there the homage ends;
A mortal quite unfit for fortune's strife,
Yet oft the sport of all the ills of life;
Prone to enjoy each pleasure riches give,
Yet happy wanting wherewithal to live,
Longing to wipe each tear, to heal each groan,
Yet frequent all unheeded in his own.

In his poem of "The Twa Dogs," what a
fine picture he draws of the different states
of society. As each is a representative of
his class, they must be introduced to the
reader:

The first I'll name—they ca'd him Cæsar—
Was keepit for his Honor's pleasure;
His hair, his size, his mouth, his lugs,
Shew'd he was nane of Scotland's dogs,
But whalpet some place far abroad,
Where sailors gang to fish for cod,
His lock lettered bran brass collar
Showed him a gentleman and scholar.

The tither was a plowman's collie,
A rhyming, ranting, raving billie,
Wha for his friends e'er comrade had him,
And in his freaks had Luath ca'd him,
After some dog in Highland sang,
Was made lang syne—Lord knows how lang—
Whyles scoured awn in lang excursion

An worried ither in diversion,
Until wi' daffin weary grown
Upon a knowl they sat them down,
And there began a lang digression
About the lords of the creation.

CÆSAR :—

I've often wondered, honest Luath,
What sort of life poor dogs like you have·
An' when the gentry's life I saw,
What way poor bodies lived ava.

LUATH :—

There nae sae wretched ane wud think,
Tho' constantly on povetith's brink,
There sae accustomed wi' the sight,
The view o't give them little fright.

As bleak-faced Hallomas returns,
They get the jovial ranting kirns,

When rural life o' ev'ry station
Unite in common recreation,
Love blinks, wit slaps, an social mirth
Forgets there's care upon the earth,
That merry day the year begins,
They bar the door on frosty winds,
The happy recks wi' mantling ream,
And sheds a heart inspiring steam;
The luntin pipe and sneeshin mill
Are handed round wi' right good will;
The cantie old folks crackin' crouse,
The young ones ranting thro' the house—
My heart has been so fain to see them
That I for joy hae barkit wi' them.
But will ye tell me, Master Cæsar,
Sure great folks live a life of pleasure?
Nae cauld nor hunger e'er can steer them,
The very thought o't need na fear them.

CÆSAR :—

L'd man, but were ye wyles where I am,

The gentles ye wad ne'er envy them;
It's true they need na starve or sweat,
Thro' winter's cauld or summer's heat,
They've nae sair work to craze their banes,
An fill auld age wi' grips an' granes,
But human bodies are sic fools,
For a' their colleges and schools,
That when their real ills perplex them,
They make enow themselves to vex them,
An ay, the less they hae to sturt them,
In like proportion less will hurt them;
Their days insipld dull and tasteless,
Their nights unquiet, lang and restless,
The ladies arm-in-arm in clusters,
As great and gracious a' as sisters;
But hear their absent thoughts of ither,
They're a run deils an gods thegither.
Whyles o'er the wie bit cup and platie,
They sip the scandal potion pretty,
Or lie lang nights wi crabbit leuks,
Pore owre the deil's pictured beuks,

> Stake on a chance the farmer's stack-yard
> An cheat like any unhanged blackguard.
>
> There's some exception, man and woman,
> But this is gentry's life in common.

Burns was a being of the strongest and most intense passion. For pretention and insincerity, bigotry and assumption, his muse had ever a scathing denunciation:

> God knows I'm not the thing I should be,
> Nor am I even the thing I could be
> But twenty times I rather would be
>> An athiest clean,
> Than under gospel colors hid be
>> Just for a screen.

Another extract from a poem, the title of which is inadmissable to ears polite, is often quoted:

O wad some pow'r the giftie gie us
To see oursels as others see us!
It wad frae monie a blunder free us,
      And foolish notion.
What airs in dress and gait wad lea'e us,
      And e'en devotion.

On diversity of condition, he says:

Some lucky find a flowing spot,
For which they never toiled nor swat;
They drink the sweet and eat the fat,
      But care or pain,
And happly eye the barren hut,
      With high disdain.

The susceptibility of Burns to female attraction, made him a popular songster, but to only one is there any true or poetical sentiment inscribed. To all except

Highland Mary it was a simple description of the charms of rural beauty. In her early death and their solemn parting on the banks of the Ayr, the poet seems to have expressed the deepest feelings of which his nature was capable, in language so chaste and beautiful that it is almost impossible to read them without a corresponding sympathy.

There is a beautiful little incident recorded of Burns' first introduction to Walter Scott, which should be perpetuated: Our poet was dining with some literary people, and observing some fine poetry written underneath a picture on the wall, he inquired the author. No one could answer, until at length a modest, fair-haired youth of fifteen, with a high intellectual forehead, and thoughtful expression of face, gave the name of Langehorne as the writer.   Burns turned and smiled upon the lad with a look which he never forgot. That boy was Walter Scott.

It has been regretted that he wrote so much in a language adapted to the peasantry. It must not be forgotten that his muse was of the clay-built cottage, and not of lordly halls. Had his descent or lineage been higher, had he not been the noble brother of the poor and lowly, so great would not have been their consolation and their pride. If his friends or favorites were of the humbler walks of life they did not long remain there—he elevated them, says a biographer to "Lauras and Saccharissas," and not only them, but their accessories shone anew, gilded by the poet's power.

His description of the "Cotter's Saturday Night" is a beautiful exmplification:

'The toil-worn cotter frae his labor goes,
This night his weekly moil is at an end,
Collects his spades, his mattocks and his hoes,
Hoping the morn in ease and rest to spend,
And weary o'er the moor his course does homeward
    bend.

At length his lowly cot appears in view
Beneath the shelter of an aged tree,
The expectant wee things toddlin stacher thro',
To meet their dad wi' flechterin' noise and glee,
His wee bit ingle blinkin' bonnily.
His clean hearth-stane, his thriftier wifie's smile,
The lisping infant prattling on his knee,
Does a' his weary carking cares beguile,
An' makes him quite forget his labor an' his toil.

Wi' joy unfeigned brothers and sisters meet,
And each for other's welfare kindly speirs,
The social hours swift-winged unnotic'd fleet,
Each tells the uncos that he sees or hears,
The parents, partial, eye their hopeful years,
Anticipation forward points the view.
The mother wi' her needle an' her shears,
Gars auld claes look amaist as weel's the new,
The father mixes a wi' admonition true.

But hark! a rap comes gently at the door,
Jenny, what kens the meaning o' the same,
Tells how a neebor lad came o'er the moor
To do some errands and convey her hame,
The wily mother sees the conscious flame
Sparkle in Jenny's e'e and flush her cheek,
With heart-struck anxious cares, inquires his name,
While Jenny bafflin's is afraid to speak,
Weel pleased the mother hears its nae wild worth-
    less rake.

There is a pleasing little incident told of Burns in connection with this poem. It is said that, with his manuscript in his hand, he went into a cottage where the gude wife was plying her wheel. He bade her stop and hearken while he read his story. She listened very patiently to the reading, and then exclaimed : "Hoot, awee, Bobbie, is not that what we all know?" The proof of its naturalness was complete— it was all he desired.

From the frequent recurrence of many biographers to the want of conjugal happiness in the household of Burns, we are apt to get the idea that his home life was clouded. This was only so when poverty, with its inconveniences, intervened. He himself says: " I have never seen where I could make a better choice of a wife." Her devotion as wife and mother appears deserving of every praise. It was thought the death of his child, a lovely girl of tender years, hastened his own. Almost his last effort was the letter he wrote his brother. He said: "I am dangerously ill, and not likely to get better. God keep my wife and children." His premonitions were correct. Fever, delirium and debility finished a life which had rapidly decayed beneath the delicate peculiarities that belong to the temperament of genius, and accordingly, at the early age of thirty-eight, Scotland mourned her brilliant and gifted son.

A few lines expressive of his affection for his wife also shows his devotional tendency:

19

O all ye powers who rule above,
O Thou whose very self art love,
  Thou know'st my words sincere;
The life-blood streaming through my heart,
Or my more dear immortal part,
  Is not more fondly dear.
When heart-corroding care and grief
  Deprive my soul of rest,
Her dear idea brings relief
  And solace to my breast.
   Thou Being all-seeing,
   O hear my fervent prayer,
   Still take her and make her
   Thy most peculiar care.

Another evidence that he still in his better moods remembered the religious training of his youth, and wearied with the disappointments and false promises of friends, his spirit longed for rest, is given in the annexed beautiful poem:

THE LAND O' THE LEAL.

I'm wearin' awa', Jean
Like sma'—wraiths in tha', Jean,
I'm wearin' awa'
      To the Land o' the Leal.

There's nae sorrow there, Jean,
There's nither could mair care, Jean,
The days are a' fair
      I' the Land o' the Leal.

O dry your gistening e'e, Jean,
My soul langs to be free, Jean,
And angels beckon me
      To the Land o' the Leal.

Ye have been gude an' true, Jean,
Your task's near ended noo, Jean,
And I'll welcome you
      To the Land o' the Leal.

Our bonny bairn's there, Jean,
She was baith gude and fair, Jean,
And we grudged her sair
      To the Land o' the Leal.

MOTHERWELL.

If William Motherwell had never written but the poem of Jeanie Morrison, it would have gained for him an immortality. He has been compared to Burns in his exquisite tenderness and pathos. Like him, he was at one time a violent partizan and an uncompromising politician; but when years have passed away the petty interests of a local sphere are lost, with all their elements of bitterness and hatred. The beautiful sentiments of Jeanie Morrison will weave an imperishable chaplet for the brow of him who lives in this touching and pure record of a faithful heart. Of this poem it has been said "that while the charming song appears like an irrepressible gush of feeling that would find vent, yet its finish was the result not of a curious felicity, but of the nicest elaboration." By touching and retouching during many years, did Jeanie Morrison attain her perfection. If the reader will but have patience with the peculiar dialect, he will find himself amply repaid in its perusal:

I've wandered east, I've wandered west,
  Through mony a weary way;
But never, never can forget
  The luve o' life's young day;
The fire that's blown on Beltan's e'en
  May weel be black gin Yule,
But blacker fa awaits the heart
  Where first fond luve grows cule.

O dear, dear Jeanie Morrison,
  The thochts o' bygane years
Still fling their shadows ower my path,
  And blend my e'en wi' tears;
They blind my e'en wi' saut, saut tears,
  And sair and sick I pine,
As memory idly summons up
  The blithe blinks o' lang syne.

'Twas then we luvit ilk ither weel
  'Twas then we twa did part,
Sweet time, sad time, twa bairns at schule,
  Twa bairns and but ae heart.
'Twas then we sat on ae laigh bink,
  To lui ilk ither lear,
And tones and looks and smiles were shed,
  Remembered ever mair.

I wonder, Jeanie, often yet,
  When sitting on that bink,
Cheek touchin' cheek, loop locked in loop,
  What our wee heads could think;

When baith ben down, ower ae braid page,
  Wi' ae buik on our knee;
Thy lips were on thy lesson, but
  My lesson was in thee.

Oh, mind ye how we hung our heads,
  How cheeks brent red wi' shame,
Whene'er the schule weans laughin' said
  We clecked thegither hame
And mind ye o' the Saturdays
  (The schule then skaill at noon),
When we ran off to speel the braes,
  The broomy braes o' Juue.

My head rins round and round about,
  My heart flows like a sea,
As ane by ane the thochts rush back,
  O' schule time and o' thee.
O mornin' life! O mornin' luve!
  O lichsome days and lang,
When hinnied hopes around our hearts
  Like simmer blossoms, sprang!

O mind ye, luve, how aft we left
  The deavin' dinsome toun,
To wander by the green burnside,
  And hear its water croon?
The simmer leaves hung owre our heads,
  The flowers burst 'round our feet,
And in the gloamin' o' the wud
  The throssil 'whusslit sweet.

The throssil whusslit in the wud,
  The burn sung to the trees,
And we with Nature's heart in tune,
  Concerted harmonies;
And on the knowe abune the burn,
  For hours thegither sat
In the silentness o' joy, till baith
  Wi' vera gladness grat!

Aye, aye, dear Jeanie Morrison,
  Tears trinkled doun your cheek,
Like dew-beads on a rose, yet nane
  Had ony power to speak!

That was a time, a blessed time,
  When hearts were fresh and young,
When freely gushed all feelings forth,
  Unsyllabled—unsung ;

I marvel, Jeanie Morrison,
  Gin I hae been to thee
As closely twined wi' earliest thochts
  As ye hae been to me ?
Oh ! tell me gin their music fills
  Thine ear as it does mine ;
Oh ! say gin e'er your heart grows grit
  Wi' dreamings o' lang syne ?

I've wandered east, I've wandered west,
  I've borne a weary lot ;
But in my wanderings, far or near,
  Ye never were forgot.
The fount that first burst frae this heart,
  Still travels on its way ;
And channels deeper as it rins,
  The luve o' life's young day.

O dear, dear Jeanie Morrison,
　Since we were sundered young,
I've never seen your face, nor heard
　The music of your tongue;
But I could hug all wretchedness,
　And happy could I dee,
Did I but ken your heart still dreamed
　O' bygane days and me!

Another Scotch poem of striking beauty of description is " Cumnor Hall," doubly interesting from the impression which it made on Walter Scott. He says " the first stanza especially had a peculiar charm to my fancy, and I found myself repeating it again and again." To it the world is probably indebted for Kenilworth. Although too long to be inserted in full, it is too fine a specimen of its author's style to be lightly regarded. Walter Scott found it in

"Evan's Ancient Ballads," and ascribed it
to Mickle:

The dews of summer night did fall,
  The moon (sweet regent of the sky)
Silvered the walls of Cumnor Hall,
  And many an oak that grew thereby.

Now nought was heard beneath the skies
  (The sounds of busy life were still),
Save an unlucky lady's sighs,
  That issued from that lonely pile.

"Leicester," she cried, "is this thy love
- That thou so oft has sworn to me,
To leave me in this lonely grove,
  Immured in shameful privacy?

No more thou com'st with lover's speed,
  Thy once beloved bride to see;
But be she alive, or be she dead,
  I fear, stern Earl, 's the same to thee.

Not so the usage I received
  When happy in my father's hall;
No faithless husband then me grieved,
  No chilling fears did me appal.

I rose up with the cheerful morn,
  No lark so blithe, no flower so gay;
And, like the bird that haunts the thorn,
  So merrily sung the live-long day.

If that my beauty is but small,
  Among court ladies all despised,
Why did'st thou rend it from that hall,
  Where, scornful Earl, it well was prized.

And when you first to me made suit,
  How fair I was, you oft would say!
And, proud of conquest, plucked the fruit,
  Then left the blossom to decay.

*   *   *   *   *   *   *

Thus lone and sad that lady grieved
  In Cumnor Hall, so lone and drear;
And many a heartfelt sigh she heaved,
  And let fall many a bitter tear.

And ere the dawn of day appeared,
  In Cumnor Hall, so lone and drear,
Full many a piercing scream was heard,
  And many a cry of mortal fear.

*   *   *   *   *   *

Full many a traveller has sighed,
  And pensive wept the Countess' fall,
As wandering onwards they've espied
  The haunted towers of Cumnor Hall.

SUGGESTED BY PAYNE'S PICTURE OF " THE AVE MARIA."

Ave Maria, from yon convent gray,
　The evening bell is calling us to prayer,
Its mellowed chimes in distance fade away,
　Parting the stillness of the summer air.
Ave Maria at this holy hour,
　When the deep fountains of the heart are stirred,
'Tis sweet to feel the plentitude of power,
　Which God on thee conferred.

Oh holy mother, by thy blessed aid,
　We hope on earth to do our Saviour's will,
Oh light the shadows on our path-way laid,
　And holy confidence with peace instil;
Then shall that watchful care, that brooding love,
　Prevail to save us when the tempter's nigh,
Blessed in thy guidance ne'er again we'll rove,
　But mount successive to thy throne on high.

That bell hath warned us like some gentle tone,
  A voice of pleading ne'er to be forgot,
Resistless monitor, can there be one
  Who to thy summons answers not?
Yon gentle maid, Italia's dark-eyed child,
  Has laid aside the swift propelling oar,
Her boat lies moveless on the sunny wave,
  To heaven and thee her orisons now soar.

Oh favored land, no Protean faith is thine,
  No symbol veering with the summer air,
The holy type, the true suggestive sign
  That tells of Calvary alone is there.
And now, though parted from thy deep blue main,
  Thy sun-lit hills, thy far-off sounding sea,
Visions are flitting through my busy brain,
  Which stir the magic chords of memory.

The spells of home are deep within my heart,
  Its haunting memories, and its whispering tones
Of my lone life, they are the only part
  O'er which a sunbeam glimmers on.

Ave Maria, bless that hallowed spot,
  My vine-wreathed home, her smiling olive plains
Oh look with pity on my lonely lot,
  And bring the exile to his home again.

TO AN ABSENT BROTHER.

My brother, thou'rt a wanderer now,
  The deep blue sea our path divides,
But still our love shall follow thee,
  Whatever weal or woe betide.

The memories of our early days,
  Our mother's look, her tones of love,
Those gentle teachings ever blent,
  With holy themes of earth above.

These yearning thoughts oft bring thee back,
  For wert thou not a sharer too,
In many a low-breathed pray'r that fell
  Upon our paths like glistening dew.

20

That mother's form hath passed away,
   But not the memories which endear,
Or else when but her name is spoke,
   Why thickly course the blinding tears.

Then think be thine a sunny path,
   Or one of dangers lone and wild,
That from the heaven her love hath won,
   Our mother bends to bless her child.

MERRY CHRISTMAS.

"Merry Christmas! Merry Christmas!" How sweetly sounds the old time-honored salutation, bringing us back to days of yore, when the fondest dream of our juvenility was to anticipate the good old Santa Claus. How often we wondered at his magical ubiquity, yet never for one moment doubting the tales of our good old nurse, of the ponies prancing down the chimney, of the stockings being filled in a trice, of the justly proportioned rewards to each and all. Happy, happy days of innocent childhood—after years, with their more refined pleasures, can never compensate for the sweet delusions of youth.

Beautifully has one of our own poets described this festival in the days of "Merry England," in those days " when nature gave her ample store." In " this wise sang he:"

"Within the halls are song and laughter,
  The cheeks of Christmas grow red and jolly,
And sprouting is every corbel and rafter
  With the lightsome green of ivy and holly.
Through the deep gulf of the chimney wide
Wallows the yule-log's roaring tide."

I question much if the iconoclastic march of progress can make up for what we have lost in the genial heartiness of the Anglo-Saxon's mode of celebration. May we never grow too wise for Merry Christmas; and though often, very often in the vicissitudes of life, it brings to us with tenfold bitterness the memory of the loved and lost, for at such times the heart ever goes back to renew alike its grief and love, on the altar of affection. Still must we say :

"Hail to thee! season of joy and festivity,
  Social pleasures and innocent mirth,
Which smooth the path of age's declivity, .
  And render to infancy Eden on earth."

*   *   *   *   *   *

Ring, ring the bells a merry peal,
  Let loud hosannas fill the air,
This day is born our Saviour king,
  Then banish every grief and care.

This day from Heaven's bright throne He came,
  To dwell on earth a simple babe,
His mother's arms are round Him thrown,
  And on her breast His head is laid.

His rosy lips are joining hers
   In many a holy, fervent kiss,
The tears of love are on His cheek,
   Her heart is filled with rapturous bliss.

Then trim the halls with ivy green,
   And let the yule log away.
Be blithe and happy every one,
   To welcome in the Christmas day.

OLIVER GOLDSMITH.

Oliver Goldsmith, although he ranks as an English poet, was born at a place called Pallas, in the county of Longford, Ireland. His father was an humble curate, and "passing rich, with forty pounds a year." Although in humble circumstances, the family had their share of ancestral pride, and boasted not a little of an honorable Spanish descent. The name of Goldsmith was adopted in the sixteenth century, and was derived from the mother's side. It is said much of the romantic and wandering character which distinguished Goldsmith's after years was imbibed from the early teaching

of his school-master, who had been an offi-
cer in the wars of Queen Anne, and who,
finding in his young charge a ready listener,
poured into his willing ears the wild and
thrilling adventures of which he was often
the hero. Oliver's talents having attracted
the notice of some relatives of the
family, who, knowing the narrow circumstances of his father offered to send him
to school, now commenced the troubles of
his life. Being naturally sprightly and gay,
he upon one occasion imprudently invited
some persons of both sexes to his rooms for
a little entertainment. His tutor, who was
a man of choleric temperament, chastised
young Goldsmith in the presence of his
friends. This disgrace drove him for a time
from the university, but, matters being ami-
cably arranged, he returned afterwards, and

finished his course ; but it was remarkable that he did not fulfill the expectations of his friends, nor develop the promise of his boyhood. From his first situation as tutor he saved about £30, with which he bought a horse and commenced his rambles through the country. After some weeks he returned home with a miserable nag, which he called Fiddleback. His story was, he had sold his first horse to pay his passage for America, but while he was viewing the curiosities of the town the ship sailed, and he had just sufficient left to purchase the wretched animal he bestrode. His uncle, who was always kind and lenient to his faults, sent him to the temple. On his way to London he was fleeced by some gamesters and returned shortly, in disgrace, to his mother. Again his friends assist him. Next we find

him in Edinburgh studying medicine. After
attending several courses he started for
Leyden, where, with his usual improvidence,
we discover him spending the last farthing
in purchasing some costly roots for a friend.
He set out now on the tour of Europe,
without money; but with his flute he won
the hearts of the peasantry, for their hospitality followed, as he says in The Traveler,
which is a description of his journey:

"How often have I led thy sportive choir
With tuneless pipe, beside the murmuring Loire,
Where shading elms along the margin grew,
And freshened from the wave the zephyr flew;
And haply though my harsh touch, faltering still,
But mocked all tune and marred the dancer's skill,
Yet would the village praise my wondrous power
And dance forgetful of the noontide hour.
Alike all ages; dames of ancient days

Have led their children through the mirthful maze,
And the gay grandsire, skilled in gestic lore.
Has frisked beneath the burden of three score."

The employments of Goldsmith were as various as his writings. He was usher in an academy, a journeyman chemist, a contributor to Dr. Griffith's Monthly Review, and a conductor of the Lady's Magazine. As a writer, he was historian, essayist, philosopher and poet. His fortunes were as various as his occupations. The sad description which he gives of An Author's Bedchamber was no doubt drawn from his own life experience:

" The muse found Scraggon stretched beneath a rug;
A window patched with paper lent a ray
That dimly showed the state in which he lay;
The sanded floor that grits beneath the tread;

The humid wall with paltry pictures spread;
The royal game of Goose was there in view,
And the twelve rules the royal martyr drew;
The seasons framed with listing found a place,
And brave Prince William showed his lamp black
    face;
The morn was cold; he views with keen desire
The rusty gate unconscious of a fire;
With beer and milk arrears the frieze was scored
And five cracked teacups dressed the chimney board;
A night-cap decked his brows instead of bay,
A cap by night—a stocking all the day!"

When hard at work earning the scanty pittance which furnished this wretched life, he spent every spare penny on the poor children who were his neighbors, and as one of his biographers tells us, " taught them dancing by way of cheering their poverty." He was known far and near by the poor, who regarded him as their own, and many an interesting and noble trait of his generous character is recorded in the fond appellation which they familliarly bestowed upon him of "our doctor." In his Deserted Village, which is considered his best work, how feelingly he portrays the sad condition of the poor:

"She, wretched matron, forced in age for bread,
To strip the brook with mantling cresses spread,
To pick her wintry faggot from the thorn,
To seek her nightly shed and weep till morn;
She only left of all the harmless train,
The sad historian of the pensive plain."

There is a quiet beauty, an intellectual composure blending with the chaste simplicity of Goldsmith, and we feel often, after reading his descriptions and observations,

no one else could have written so well.
Read his indignant exclamation against
lordly luxury and monotonous pleasure,
which, as Campbell observes, " aped the
grandeur of the feudal ages, without its
hospitality," and indignantly spurned the
cottage from the green. Hear his description of the migration to a distant shore :

"And sorrows deep that gloomed the parting day
Which called them from their native walks away;
When the poor exiles, every pleasure past,
Hung round the bowers and fondly looked their last,
And took a long farewell, and wished in vain
For scenes like these beyond the western main;
And shuddering still to face the distant deep,
Returned and wept, and still returned to weep.
The good old sire the first prepared to go
To new found worlds, and wept for others' woe;
But for himself in conscious virtue brave,

He only wished for worlds beyond the grave.
His lovely daughter, lovelier in her tears,
The fond companion of his helpless years,
Silent went next, neglectful of her charms,
And left a lover's for a father's arms.
With louder plaints the mother spoke her woes,
And blest the cot where every pleasure rose,
And kissed her thoughtless babes with many a tear
And clasped them close in sorrow doubly dear;
Whilst her fond husband strove to lend relief
In all the silent manliness of grief."

How little does the poet draw from fancy that can pen such a picture. How closely has he confined himself to realities. There is a true pathos, a tender lament, in the sympathy which he expresses that our own heart echoes, and the poet commands us at his will. The Traveller was Goldsmith's first successful attempt in the world of letters. It passed rapidly through several editions. Dr. Johnson has declared it too discursive; but it was a simple sketch of his itinerant life, and his descriptions vary with the countries which he describes. The superior results of his mode of observing men and manners is evidenced by the success of his work:

"From that land where France displays her bright
    domain
To men of other minds my fancy flies,
Embosomed in the deep where Holland lies.
Methinks her patient sons before me stand,
Where the broad ocean leans against the land,
And sedulous to stop the coming tide,
Lift the tall rampire's artificial pride.
Onward methinks and diligently slow,
The firm connected bulwark seems to grow;
Spreads its long arms amidst the watery roar,

Scoops out an empire and usurps the shore:
While the pent ocean rising o'er the pile,
Sees an amphibious world beneath him smile;
The slow canal, the yellow-blossomed vale,
The willow-tufted bank, the gliding sail,
The crowded mart, the cultivated plain,
A new creation rescued from his reign."

In a letter of dedication to his brother, Goldsmith says: "I have endeavored to show that there may be equal happiness in States that are differently governed from our own: that every State has a particular principle of happiness, and that this principle in each may be carried to a mischievous excess, there are few can judge better than yourself." The Traveller is dedicated to this, his favorite brother, of whom he says:

"Where'er 1 roam, whatever realms to see,
My heart untravell'd fondly turns to thee;
Still to my brother turns with ceaseless pain,
And drags at each remove a lengthening chain." -

The "Amor Patriæ" was never more fitly described than in the following, taken from the same poem :

"But where to find the happiest spot below,
Who can direct when all pretend to know?
The shuddering tenant of the frigid zone
Boldly proclaims that happiest spot his own;
Extols the treasures of his stormy seas,
And his long nights of revelry and ease;
The naked negro panting at the line
Boasts of his golden sands and palmy wine,
Basks in the glare or stems the tepid wave,
And thanks his gods for all the good they gave—
Such is the patriot's boast where'er we roam,
His first best country ever is at home."

The steady popularity of Goldsmith in that era of literature when pretension was easily unmasked, and when the standard was

supported by men of genius and scholarship, is indeed a consideration not to be
overlooked. When the mind is bewildered,
when the brain aches by the sensation im-
probabilities, the startling incidents, the
terrific disclosures of our every day fictions,
our highly wrought pictures of fashionable
and false life, turn to the " Vicar of Wakefield." It appears, indeed, like the record
(as it truly is) of another age. Its lessons
of rural life and humble virtue, its simple
credulity and unsophisticated innocence are
charming in their very freshness. There
is not even an attempt at mystery, except
in one character. Goldsmith did not cater
to that taste which is only satisfied by
something out of the entire order of natural
events, and which make vice not the mon-
ster of hideous mien, but a poor suffering

martyr to circumstances, while honest, plain homespun virtue is simply tolerated, seldom reverenced and honored.

The sale of the Vicar of Wakefield brought our poet £60. It came most opportunely —just at that time when he was immured within by bailiffs, and threatened to be driven out by his long-suffering landlady. Shortly after this publication he became recognized in good society, and was the recipient of much literary distinction. He also became a member of some clubs only frequented by men of genius, and many a pungent witticism and brilliant sally is recorded of those convivial reunions. Many forgotten (save at the passing moment) have passed silently away into the oblivion of time,—others found their way out, and live as pictures of the past. It was proposed

one evening, when Goldsmith happened to
be absent, to write his epitaph. It was ac·
cordingly done, and he was called upon for
an answer. This is the history of his some·
what celebrated poem " Retaliation."

At the next meeting he sent in the fol·
lowing :

Of old when Scarron his companions invited,
Each guest brought his dish, and the feast was united.
If our landlord supplies us with beef and with fish,
Let each guest bring himself, and he brings the best
    dish :
Our Dean shall be ven'son just fresh from the plains,
Our Burke shall be tongue with a garnish of brains,
Our Will shall be wild fowl of excellent flavor,
And Dick with his pepper shall heighten the savor,
Our Cumberland's sweet bread its place shall obtain,
And Douglas is pudding substantial and plain ;
Our Garrick's a salad, for in him, we see,
Oil, vinegar, sugar and saltness agree ;

To make out the dinner full certain I am
That Ridge is anchovy, and Reynolds is lamb,
That Hickey's a capon, and by the same rule
Magnanimous Goldsmith a goosberry fool.
At a dinner so various, at such a repast,
Who'd not be a glutton and stick to the last?
Here, waiter, more wine, let me sit while I'm able,
Till all my companions sink under the table;
Then with chaos and blunder encircling my head
Let me ponder and tell what I think of the dead.
Here lies the good Dean reunited to earth,
Who mixed reason with pleasure, and wisdom with
     mirth.

Here lies our good Edmund whose genius was such
We scarcely can praise it or blame it too much;
Who, born for the universe, narrowed his mind,
And to party gave up what was meant for mankind.
Here lies David Garrick—describe him who can;
An abridgement of all that was pleasant in man;
As an actor, confessed without rival to shine;
As a wit, if not first, in the very first line.

Here Hickey reclines, a most pleasant, blunt creature,
And slander itself must allow him good nature;
He cherished his friend, and he relished a bumper,
Yet one fault he had, and that was a thumper!
Perhaps you may ask if the man was a miser;
I answer no, no; for he always was wiser;
Too courteous, perhaps, or obligingly flat?
His very worst foe can't accuse him of that;
Perhaps he has confided in men as they go,
And so was too foolishly honest? Ah, no.
Then what was his failing? come, tell it and burn ye;
He was—could he help it?—a " special attorney."

Here Reynolds is laid, and to tell you my mind,
He has not left a wiser or better behind;
His pencil was striking, resistless and grand;
His manners were gentle, complying and bland;
Still born to improve us in every part,
His pencil our faces, his manners our heart;
To coxcombs averse, yet most civilly steering,
When they judg'd without skill he was still hard of
    hearing.

When they talked of their Raphaels, Corregios and
    stuff,
He shifted his trumpet* and only took snuff.

Strange with all his originality and refinement of mind, Goldsmith should have
been the subject of witticism. His country
dialect and person were kept in view by
ignorant witlings, while his noble qualities
were often overlooked. He was almost ever
a loser in conversation, and Johnson re-
marked of him, "no man was more foolish
when he had not a pen in his hand, or more
wise when he had," and he further observes
"whatever he composed he did it better
than any other man could, and whether we
consider him as a poet, a comic writer, or a
historian, (so far as regards his powers of

---

*Sir Joshua Reynolds was so remarkably deaf as to be under the
necessity of using an ear trumpet in company.

composition,) he was one of the first writers of his time, and will ever stand in the foremost class." Strange indeed with such rare endowments there should be joined such unperverted simplicity, such delight in the delineation of humble life. He could write Roman and English histories, biographies and introductions to books, a history of the earth and animated nature, and—

—he could stoop to trace
The parlor splendors of that place;
The white washed wall, the sanded floor,
The varnish'd clock that clicked behind the door;
The chest contrived a double debt to pay,
A bed by night, a chest of drawers by day;
The pictures placed for ornament and use,
The twelve good rules, the royal game of goose,
The hearth, except when winter chilled the day,
With aspen boughs, and flowers, and fennel gay,
While broken teacups, wisely kept for show,
'Ranged o'er the chimney, glistened in a row.

The very truthfulness of Goldsmith's character, which prevented him from dissembling or hiding his emotions, led to many a rebuke from the stately and pedantic Johnson. At one time when complaining of the unjustness of some epithet which had been bestowed upon him, Johnson exclaimed, "poh! poh! doctor; let them call you Holofernes if they like, what matters it?" and when he experienced some chagrin at the reception which his "Man in Black" received, he showed the most unmitigated contempt for "poor Goldy," as he styled him in derision, that he should feel or care. The truth is, although Goldsmith had known and suffered much, he had not lived so long in poverty as his great contemporary, "nor suffered so long from hope deferred." Johnson was over fifty when he was first known to the public ; Goldsmith only forty-six when he died.

As mannerism makes the identity of distinguished individuals, so, although oftentimes odd and even offensive, we learn to regard it as sacred, being a part of themselves. Milton, Burke, and Johnson most of all was remarkable for this. Goldsmith said to him one day, "If you were to write a fable about little fishes, Doctor, you would make the little fishes talk like whales." A literary discussion with Johnson was delightful; yet so was a chat with the watch-maker in Gun Arbor Court, and the tailor who patched his only velvet coat so nicely. He sympathized with the wrongs of all classes; perhaps it was not his particular merit ; his heart was naturally feeling, and it was involuntary. But we must love the man who could leave a convivial party to search for some poor woman whose tones, as she chanted a ditty in passing by, indicated distress; and he rejoiced more in the exercise of those tender and noble sentiments than in the highest triumphs of scholarship and renown. He never made use of stratagem to compass a favor. At one time his friends were anxious that he should procure some patronage from the Earl of Bute. He undertook to prepare an introduction. Meeting the upper steward, he mistook him for "my lord," and gave him the benefit of what had been prepared for ears polite. He retrieved his error in his usual way, by telling the nobleman that he had no confidence in the patronage of the great, but would rather rely on the booksellers.

In judging of the sentiments of poets,

we usually allow them so much of what is called "poetic license" that a strict and logical interpretation is scarcely ever indulged in. With Goldsmith it is quite different. He keeps so close to realities, and draws certain conclusions respecting the destiny and happiness of mankind so accurately and pointedly that we judge him by a different standard, although this may be complimentary to him as a philosopher, by the same rule we may misjudge him as a poet.

It has been said his theory is averse to trade and wealth and arts. He delineates their evils, and disdains their vaunted benefits, as in the following extract:

O luxury, thou curs'd by heaven's decree,
How do thy potions with insidious joy
Diffuse their pleasures only to destroy;

Kingdoms by thee to sickly greatness grown,
Boast of a florid vigor not their own.
At every draught more large and large they grow,
A bloated mass of rank, unwieldly woe,
Till sapped their strength and every part unsound,
Down, down they sink, and spread a ruin 'round.

Goldsmith vindicates his own expressed views in a letter to Sir Joshua Reynolds. He says : " For twenty or thirty years past, it has been the fashion to consider luxury as one of the greatest national advantages; and all the wisdom of antiquity in that particular as erroneous. Still, however, I must remain a professed ancient on that head, and continue to think those luxuries prejudicial to states by which so many vices are introduced, and so many kingdoms have been undone. Indeed, so much has been poured out of late on the other side of the question, that, merely for the sake of novelty, and variety, one would sometimes wish to be right." "Truth is an endearing quality;" perhaps it was this spell that brought so many hearts to his shrine. Certain it is, he was loved while living, and mourned when dead.

When Goldsmith died, Reynolds, then in the full tide of success, threw his pencil aside in sorrow, and Burke turned from the fast brightening vision of renown to weep. No obituary more sincere or more heartfelt could be desired than this.

CHRISTMAS SONG—1866.

An anthem of joy, an anthem of love,
'For another Christmas day;
Let the earth rejoice, the Heavens be glad
While we our offerings pay.

We come with lowly, reverent hearts,
To that crib and manger old,
But not with gems and settings rare,
Of diamond and of gold.

Oh no, not these, for the earth is His,
The stars and the boundless sea,
The moon that gems the vaulted dome,
In her silvery canopy.

An angel band at His behest,
  The couriers of His will,
Await the mandate which shall bid
  The unceasing world bo still.

On earth so weak, in Heaven so strong,
  A mortal yet divine,
.I ask not, for I may not know
  This mystery of thine.

Then an anthem of love, an anthem of joy,
  For our Saviour's natal day,
With the angel choir exulting join,
  The sweet attesting lay.

TO M. H

—

Dear friend, dear friend, my heart to day
Renews its youth from memory's spring,
And as its rolling waters play,
One gift to you it fain would bring.

My mother's friend! That name alone
Must bind thee ever to my heart;
My guide through many a dreary waste—
Such thou hast been, and still thou art.

My wilful pride, my wayward youth,
Defied reproof from all but thee;
Thy soothing love, thy kindly blame,
Hath made whatever good there be.

Then as ye cluster round the board,
And as ye quaff the goodly cheer,
Oh take my love, my fondest wish,
For blessings on the coming year.

THE AUTUMN RAMBLE.

Come my darlings for a ramble,
  To the woods so dun and sere,
Don your cloaks and tie your bonnets,
  For the morn is cold and clear.

Glows each face with expectation,
  For the treasures to be found,
Nuts and cones, with pretty acorns,
  Strewed upon the leafy ground.

Don and Dash are on before us,
  Bounding merrily up the hill,
Looking back with furtive glances
  Barking their impatient will.

Shall we to the grove of cedars,
  Winter there is ever green,
And the sun with side-long glances
  Flings to earth a paler sheen.

Nay, reluctant, you would rather
  To the beechen woods below,
Where we found the dark green fern leaves
  Only a few days ago.

Now with little hands close pressing,
  Tender palms love-linked in mine,
Pattering feet to laughing measure,
  Happy glides the merry time.

DR. JOHNSON.

DR. SAMUEL JOHNSON was born on the 18th of September, 1709, at Lichfield, in Staffordshire. From neither father nor mother had he any great amount of intellect to inherit. Their extraction was obscure. His father is represented as being an unwavering devotee to the house of Stuart, and strongly prejudiced in favor of their cause. He was a bookseller and stationer in Derbyshire. His mother, with a mind unimproved by education, was nevertheless a woman of good natural understanding, eminently pious and conscientious according to her standard of religious faith, and her son in after years acknowledged, with gratitude and almost veneration, the benefits of her early instruction. The effects of the many castigations Johnson received at school from his severe but attentive teacher, influenced him in favor of a free use of the rod, and in all his conversations on the subject he declared strenuously in favor of the same. He commanded respect from his school-fellows by his remarkable proficiency and aptitude ; it always exceeded his apparent diligence, but, in truth, when he seemed idle he was often laboring. Dr. Adams said of him : "No young man ever entered the university better qualified." In order to defray his expenses there he became companion to a gentleman of Shropshire, who spontaneously undertook to support him. Among his companions he was looked up to as a man of wit and spirit, but he was always subject to fits of melancholy (which he inherited from his father), accompanied by alternate irritation and languor. From nature he had received an uncouth figure and diseased constitution, as a kind of detraction, perhaps, for his great mental abilities, for after all our common mother is not as partial in her gifts as we are apt to consider her, and her doctrine of compensation very often comes in most opportunely as an offset to repress our presumption or save us from despair. At Mr. Jordan's (his teacher's) request, he translated Pope's Messiah into Latin verse as a Christmas exercise. Shortly after leaving college his father died. The means he left were scarcely sufficient to afford a temporary support to his mother, and in the following year he accepted a situation as usher in a school; but that was rendered irksome to him from the pride and pomposity of its patron, Sir Wolstun Dixie. He finally threw up his situation in disgust, and becoming the guest of Mr. Hector (an eminent surgeon), embarked in the uncertainties of authorship. But even in these, his first works, may be observed the energetic and manly style (notwithstanding the mannerisms) which he is said to have initiated and taught his countrymen. His labors at this time were principally translations, dedications and essays. Having suggested some improvements in the management of the Gentleman's Magazine, its editor employed him as a contributor, and Johnson entered into an agreement to furnish those articles which he himself had the privilege of se-

lecting. In the following year he married
the widow of Mr. Porter, a mercer of Bir-
mingham, a lady who, although twenty years
his senior, is said to have been the object
of his first passion. From this disparity,
joined to a peculiar temper, their conjugal
happiness was not uninterrupted. But he always spoke of her respectfully, and mourned
her loss with unfeigned sorrow. With the
fortune which she brought him he fitted up
an academy. Three pupils only rewarded
his endeavors. One of these was the celebrated David Garrick, who remained ever
the devoted friend of Johnson. Their fortunes were as different as their peculiar
abilities. Garrick, as is well known, devoted
himself to the stage, and receiving its
highest honors, retired on a fortune splendid beyond all precedent for an actor ;

while Johnson struggled on, in poverty and comparative obscurity, for many a weary year. At the end of six months the school was declared a failure, and given up. His "London," an imitation of the third satire of Juvenal, won for Dr. Johnson the famo and respect of his contemporaries, and it was said, "the writer of so fine a poem cannot long remain unknown." He compares and contrasts the pleasures of a rural life with that of a city.

> There none are swept by sudden fate away,
> But all whom hunger spares, with age decay;
> Here malice, rapine, accident, conspire,
> And now a rabble rages, now a fire;
> Their ambush here relentless ruffians lay,
> And here the fell attorney prowls for prey;
> Here falling houses thunder on your head,
> And here a female atheist talks you dead.

His prejudice against France and Spain finds here a convenient outlet, and he deplores the introduction of those manners and occupations which might effeminate or degrade the more manly Briton. Imagining the effects he fears, he says :

Nor hope the British lineaments to trace,
The rustic grandeur or the surly grace,
But lost in thoughtless ease and empty show,
Behold the warrior dwindled to a beau ;
Sense, freedom, piety, refined away,
Of France the mirror and of Spain the prey;
All that at home no more can beg or steal,
Or like a gibbet better than a wheel,
Hissed from the stage or hooted from the court,
Their air, their dress, their politics import;
Obsequious, artful, voluble and gay,
On Britain's fond credulity they prey,

*　　*　　*　　*　　*　　*

Turn from this to the description of character. It would seem as if all the acerbity of Johnson was excited against

> The supple Gaul who, born a parasite,
> Still to his interest true where'er he goes,
> Wit, bravery, worth his lavish tongue bestows;
> In every face a thousand graces shine,
> From every tongue flows harmony divine,
> These arts in vain our rugged natives try,
> Strain out with faltering diffidence a lie,
> And gain a kick for awkward flattery.
> Well may they venture on the mimic's art,
> Who play from morn to night a borrowed part,
> Practis'd their masters' notions to embrace,
> Repeat his maxims and reflect his face,
> With every wild absurdity comply,
> And view each object with another's eye:
> To shake with laughter ere the jest they hear,
> To pour at will the counterfeited tear,
> And as their patron hints the cold or heat,
> To shake in dog-days, in December sweat,

> How, when competitors like these contend,
> Can surly virtue hope to find a friend ?
> Slaves that with serious impudence beguile,
> And lie without a blush, without a smile.

He who for nearly all his life had tasted poverty to its bitter dreg, had looked from its sad and lonely contemplations on the means and ends by which men " raise a palace and a manor buy," might well exclaim :

> This mournful truth is everywhere confessed,
> Slow rises worth by poverty oppressed.

Johnson, Collins, Fielding and Thomson, names the most celebrated during the eighteenth century, were all four at different times arrested for debt. The supreme power, after the accession of the house of

Hanover, passed into the hands of Sir Hor-
ace Walpole, who, whatever his talents for
government and debate, had but little taste
for authors, and that fund which, under
Bolingbroke, had fostered men of letters,
was now employed in bartering for par-
liamentary support. Macauley says, " the
coarse joke of his friend, Sir Charles Kan-
bury Williams, was more pleasing to Walpole than Thomson's Seasons or Richardson's
Pamela." Thus at the time when Johnson
commenced his literary career, a writer had
little to hope from the patronage of the
great. The season of rich harvest had
passed away, and famine now desolated the
land. All that was despicable and wretched
might be summed up in one word—*poet.*
In calamities and miseries such as these,
Johnson embarked in his twenty-eighth

year, and the information respecting him
from that period until he came before the
world with a fame established, and a pension confessed, is little indeed for the giant
of English literature. He who had so often
experienced the delusive promises of the
great might well describe, in his "Vanity
of Human Wishes," the

Unnumbered suppliants who crowd Preferment's gate,
Athirst for wealth and burning to be great
Delusive fortune hears the incessant call,
They mount, they shine, evaporate and fall
On every stage the foes of peace attend,
Hate dogs their flight and insult marks their end.
Love ends with hope; the sinking statesman's door
Pours in the morning worshipper no more;
For growing names the weekly scribbler lies,
To growing wealth the dedicator flies;
From every room descends the painted face
That hung the bright Palladium of the place,

And smoked in kitchens or in auctions sold;
To better features yields the frame of gold,
For now no more we trace in every line
Heroic worth, benevolence divine,
The form distorted justifies the fall,
And detestation rids the indignant wall.

In comparison with the great attributes
of Dr. Johnson, poetry seems quite subsi-
dary; yet his versification was ready and
free. The following, to a young lady on
her birth-day, was almost impromptu, in
the presence of Mr. Hector:

This tributary verse receive my fair,
Warm with an ardent lover's fondest prayer,
May this returning day forever find
Thy form more lovely, more adorned thy mind;
All pa'ns, all cares, may favoring heaven remove,
All but the sweet solicitude of love.
May powerful nature join with grateful art,

To point each glance, and force it to the heart;
Oh then, when conquered crowds confess thy sway,
When e'en proud wealth and prouder wit obey,
My fair, be mindful of the mighty trust,
Alas! 'tis hard for beauty to be just.

Those sovereign charms with strictest care employ,
Nor give the generous pain, the worthless joy;
With his own form acquaint the forward fool,
Shown in the mimic glass of ridicule;
Teach mimic censure her own faults to find,
No more let coquettes to themselves be blind,
So shall Belinda's charms improve mankind.

If politeness is benevolence in small things, then indeed Dr. Johnson's benevolence was confined to great things. He wanted sympathy with the common ills which generally afflict mankind. Even a great pecuniary loss failed to affect him, unless the loser were reduced to beggary. Small things appeared to him contemptible, and yet he was the slave of little habits, little tastes, little customs. Boswell tells us of his insatiable taste for tea, his extreme fondness for fish-sauce and veal-pie with plums, his trick of touching the posts as he walked, his mysterious practice of treasuring up scraps of orange peel, his morning slumbers, his midnight disputations, etc., etc., until we are able to say, with Macauley, he is better known to us than any man in history. And yet he was not wanting in affection. His beautiful poem of Rasselas was written to defray the expenses of his mother's funeral; and incredible as it may seem, Walsh tells us the whole of this elegant and philosophical fiction was prepared for press in one week, and sent in portions, as it was written. He loved his mother with the most anxious affection, and often from his scanty hoards contributed to her relief. His "Yours, without a dinner," to his bookseller, Cave, tells most powerfully the state of his impoverished finances. In a letter. to Lord Chesterfield, which is considered a model of "dignified contempt," his allusion to the loss of his wife and to his present situation is exquisitely beautiful. "The notice you have been pleased to take of my labors, had it been early, had been kind, but it has been delayed until I am indifferent and cannot enjoy it; until I am *solitary* and cannot impart it; until I am known and do not want it." Lord Chesterfield, whom Johnson regarded at one time as a liberal patron, had neglected him, but being anxious to have the dictionary, which was just finished, dedicated to him, sought to soothe him by ingenious compliments; but Johnson was indignant that his lordship would even suppose for a moment he could be reconciled by his flattery and artificial compliments. His dictionary was published in two large volumes folio. It is much to say of this work, it outlives its age, without appearance of decrepitude or decay. He issued proposals for an edition of Shakspeare, and while he was proceeding with it he was informed that the king had granted him a pension of three hundred pounds a year. He took a better house, and allotted an apartment to Mrs. Williams, a daughter of Zachary Williams, who was possessed of considerable poetic talent, but who was totally blind. Her temper was perverse and irritable, yet nothing could induce him to withdraw the charity he had once assumed. His home was often rendered unpleasant by dependents who fattened on his bounty, and yet he often said, "If I dismiss them, who will take care of them?" He was consoled for these annoyances by the friendship of the Thrale family, whose hospitality afforded him the comforts of an elegant and substantial home. An impromptu to Mrs. Thrale on the completion of her 35th year is another proof of his ready versification :

Oft in danger, yet alive,
We are come to thirty-five;
Long may better years arrive,
Better years than thirty-five.
Could philosophers contrive,
Life to stop at thirty-five,
Time his hours should never drive
O'er the bounds of thirty-five.
High to soar and deep to dive,
Nature gives at thirty-five.
Ladies, stock and tend your hive,
Trifle not at thirty-five.
For however we boast and strive,
Life declines at thirty-five.

> He that ever hopes to thrive
> Must begin at thirty-five,
> And all who wisely wish to wive
> Must look on Thrale at thirty-five.

Some of the bagatelles published in 1775 are sufficiently ridiculous, but as they afford us a vein of Johnson in a merry mood, they impart an interest. Some were written in burlesque of modern versification of ancient legendary tales, as follows:

> The tender infant, meek and mild,
>   Fell down upon the stone;
> The nurse took up the squealing child,
>   But still the child squealed on.

Another of the same kind:

> Where'er I turn my view,
> All is strange, yet nothing new,
> Endless labor all along,
> Endless labor to be wrong,

Phrase that time has flung away,
Uncouth words in disarray,
Tricked in antique ruff and bonnet,
Ode, and elegy and sonnet

One more, a parody from the translation
of the Medea of Euripides:

Err snall they not, who resolute explore
Time's gloomy backward with judicious eyes;
And scanning right the practises of yore,
Shall deem our hoar progenitors unwise.

They to the dome where smoke with curling play
Announced the dinner to the regions round,
Summoned the singer blithe and harper gay,
And aided wine with dulcet streaming sound.

The better use of notes, or sweet or shrill,
By quivering string or modulated wind,
Trumpet or lyre—to their harsh bosoms chill,
Admission ne'er had sought or could not find.

Oh, send them to the sullen mansions dun,
  Her baleful eyes where sorrow rolls around,
Where, gloom enamored, mischief loves to dwell,
  And murder, all blood boltered, schemes the wound.

Where cates the luxuriant pile the spacious dish,
  And purple nectar glads the festive hour,
The guest without a want, without a wish,
  Can yield no room to music's soothing power.

Although the success of Dr. Johnson's Shakspeare was not great at first, it increased the respect for his ability, and his talents were fully recognized by Trinity College, Dublin, from which institution he received the title of Doctor of Laws. He was in the following year admitted to a personal interview with the king, in the library of the queen's palace, and soon after was appointed professor of ancient literature. Many of

Johnson's friends, and among them Mr. Strahan, the king's printer, were anxious to procure him a seat in parliament. His biographers have made themselves merry and amused their readers not a little with conjectures as to the ridiculous figure he would have made there. His sense of right would have prevented him from being a mere party man. He very much opposed the principle that "a man should go with his party, right or wrong." "This," he once said, "is so remote from national virtue, from scholastic virtue, that a good man must have undergone a great change before he can reconcile himself to such a doctrine. It is maintaining that you may lie to the public, for you do lie when you call that right which you think wrong, or the reverse." In his "Taxation no Tyranny," he endeavored to show that distant colonies which had in their assemblies a legislature of their own, were still liable to be taxed in a British parliament, where they had no representatives, and he thought Britain was strong enough to force obedience. He afterwards felt keenly the unpopularity of his views, but would not permit himself to acknowledge the force and strength that were brought against him. At a meeting of a great number of the most respectable booksellers of London, it was unanimously agreed that an elegant and uniform edition of the English poets should be printed, with an account of the life of each author, by Dr. Samuel Johnson; and a committee accordingly waited upon him with proposals. He entered upon the task with avidity. All that was expected from him would have been embraced in a concise and succinct account of each poet, but he continued to expatiate and criticise, until at last he presented to

the world a work which could scarcely be
credited as emanating from the pen of a man
bordering on seventy. He enjoyed all the
triumphs of success in the avidity with
which his "Lives of the Poets" were read
and praised, and he did not fail to enjoy
another satisfaction, which he had always
contended a writer must expect. He was
attacked on all sides by friends of the different poets. Some contended he had said
too little, while others contended he had
said too much, as both quantity and quality
were disagreeable. During his life his opponents were sufficiently busy, but it was
astonishing how they increased in malignity
and force after his death. Concealed hostility
now showed itself even from those who had
but a short time since been voluble in his
praise. But it was his fate to receive the
just reward of his transcendent genius, re-

vered by the whole English world. His name is honored in the catalogue of her most gifted sons.

He was solemnly interred in Westminster Abbey, close by the grave of Garrick, his pupil and his friend.

AVE MARIA.

Ave Maria, the shadows are stealing,
Ave Maria, sweet anthems are pealing,
Soft while they're falling o'er earth and o'er sea,
Sweet Mary, my mother, I turn unto thee.

The zephyr is stealing ere daylight reposes,
The breath of the lily, the scent of the roses,
The birdling is hushing his gay woodland strain,
But the night-bird is chanting a sweeter refrain.

The earth is all beauty, all gladness and love,
From the world at our feet to the bright stars above,
My heart is elated such brightness to see,
And it turns in devotion, sweet mother, to thee.

HYMN OF THE NATIVITY.

Alone on Bethlehem's wooded heights
    They watched, that shepherd band of old,
Thro' the long wastes of dreary night,
    Guarding their fleecy fold.

Simple and poor, of patient faith,
    Perchance they knew not that the signs,
Long typified by prophets old,
    The ransom sprung from David's line.

Were all accomplished and the hour,
    The blissful hour at length was here,
When attestations of the truth,
    With words of promise laden cheer,

Were even now, from angel's lips,
  Vibrating on the midnight air,
But suddenly a brightness shone,
  And thro' the waves of glory there.

In sounds of softest dulcet tone,
  These words fell on the 'frighted ear,
Be not afraid, oh shepherd men,
  I bring you tidings glad to cheer.

"Good will to all and peace to men,"
  A Saviour King this day is born,
Oh, ne'er was sung so sweet a lay,
  To usher in a gladsome morn.

TO MY SISTER,

ON ENTERING A RELIGIOUS STATE.

And thou wilt go, my sister,
　From home, dear home, to dwell,
And leave those scenes of early youth
　We both have loved so well.
Thy place will soon be vacant,
　I feel it even now,
When I gaze upon thy placid face,
　Thy meek, religious brow.

I shall miss thy tender greeting,
　Thy pleasant cheerful tone,
The bounding step, the dear embrace,
　The arm around me thrown;
I shall listen for thy coming,
　Scarce believing thou art gone,
'Till grief and sadness like a pall,
　Are 'round my pathway thrown.

The future, how its shadows fall
  Upon my sinking heart,
Each passing murmur seems to breathe,
  Soon, soon, she will depart.
How lonely, oh, how lonely,
  Our father's hearth will be,
For every memory, as it floats,
  Will bring back thoughts of thee.

But it is worse than useless,
  These fond but vain regrets,
Why should my spirit anguish,
  That thine hath found its rest.
Then go, sweet sister, word of mine
  Shall never bid thee stay,
When God hath whispered to the heart,
  Its mandate is obey.

We yield thee, Lord, our treasure,
  But let this hope remain,
That in a world of changeless love,
  Our souls shall meet again.

AVE SANCTISSIMA.

Mater celorum, sweet virgin ever blest,
Ave sanctissima, oh, hear a heart oppressed;
    Guide thou thy pleading child,
        Wandering on life's stormy sea,
    Shield her with thy saving love,
        And bring her safe to thee.
    Bend down thy loving eye,
        Grant her thy pitying ear
    To thee in hope we fly,
        Oh, virgin mother hear.
    Ave mater ave,
        Hear our lonely cry,
    Sancte Mater Dei,
        Mother ever nigh.

Sancte Maria, to thee it hath been given,
Aid to lead the recreant thro' mercy's gate to
   Heaven ;
     By that holy grace conferred,
     Thro' that glorious son adored,
     Hear thou our fervent prayer.
     Mother of our Lord.

     Through the darkness of the night,
     Pray that calm our slumbers be,
     Fill our hearts with holy love,
     For Jesus and for thee.

     Ave mater ave,
     Hear our lonely cry,
     Sancte Mater Dei,
     Mother ever nigh.

CHRISTMAS MORN.

"In some parts of Germany it is a custom for aged men enveloped in long cloaks to go from house to house on Christmas morn, and announce the birth of Christ. They remind one in their appearance of the description of Palmer's, from the Holy Land." They are regarded as such in the following :

Ho, Christian knights and gentlemen, I pray ye
    listen well,
For I have traveled many a league, a story strange
    to tell,
Of one who left His Father's hall, his home and
    high estate,
The glory and the honor which no tongue could
    e'er relate.

To be an humble babe, with scarce a shelter old;

To shield his tender helplessness from misery and
cold,

No trappings He of costly silk, no. bed of cider
down,

His cradle crib a manger, upon His head no crown.

Yet monarch He of Heaven and earth, for on this
happy day,

An angel band with joy elate, proclaims the attesting
lay,

And still the burden of their song from glowing
eve till morn,

Is glory be to God on high, for Christ our King is
born.

And from a far off distant land, skilled in prophetic
lore,

With sandal shoon and scallop shell placed in each
hat before,

Three hoary men are journeying, though wearied
    they and old,
To place their treasures at His feet, of frankinsence
    and gold.

Now all good Christian people, I pray ye quick repair,
To Bethlehem, in Juda, for Christ our King is there.
Come hasten, quickly hasten, in lowliness adore,
This wondrous King and Saviour, ours for evermore.

IN MEMORIAM.

INSCRIBED TO H. C.

Farewell, farewell, 'ere Time with iron hand hath
Plowed its furrows deep upon thy brow.
With eyes undimmed by tears, with heart untouched
By sorrow's deadly blight, Death called thee hence,
And now no more at that soft hour, when love
Unites her dear ones at the household hearth,
May we greet again thy gentle presence,
Which often with its kindness bland beguil'd
The clouded brow and wearied heart to peace.
Yet faithful love is lingering still to catch,
Thro' gathering gloom, thy gladsome step and note,
So-sweet of song dear, herald of our own.
Oh, sad to think it never more may be.
The vacant chair, the missing love, too truly
Tell the home's bereavement; yet haply thou
Hast never known the weary ways of life,

Ne'er felt the anxious insecurity,
The hope deferred, nor slaked thy thirst
At Marah's fount, gathered golden hopes,
Like Dead Sea fruit, to find them ashes at
The core; and now with all the memory
Of thy early days still lingering here,
We give thee to thy God. Oh, slight the tie,
Which severs Life from Death, and flings o'er all
The sunny loveliness of youth the shadows of
The grave.

BEAUTIFUL RIVER.

Beautiful river, flowing river,
 · Ever onward to the sea,
Bear on thy foaming bosom,
 The message I fling to thee.

On, on to the trackless ocean,
 On, on to the sounding main,
Where one we love in exile
 Pines for his home again.

Tell him the silver streamlet
 From its icy bond made free,
Dances in rippling measure
 To its own sweet melody.

Tell him the clover springeth,
  The robin weaves his nest,
The tender grass is springing
  From its cold and wintry rest.

And we are wearily watching
  Adown the winding lane,
For the quickened tread, the footstep
  That cometh not again.

Now speed thee, beautiful river,
  Nor linger on thy way,
The gladness of reunion
  Brings sunshine to our day.

FAREWELL.

And now, Farewell; my pleasant task is o'er,
And dear beguilements from old memory's store,
Which solaced oftentimes a wearied hour,
Though told in simple rhymes and lacking power,
Have spoke a language which, albeit the dress,
Your gentle hearts and partial love confess,
Yet, oh, how faint, how puerile, how weak
These timid numbers which essay to speak;
The tender love, the fond desire to see,
All that a parent's heart could ask in thee.
If in the lives which I have sought to trace,
Your eyes may scan a fault which might deface,
Remember truth has bid record it all,
The genius fame and sadly oft the fall.
And now with blessings on each fair young head,
My last Farewell in fondest love is said.

FINIS.

www.ingramcontent.com/pod-product-compliance
Lightning Source LLC
Chambersburg PA
CBHW032016120726
47902CB00013B/988